D. L. LEWIS

ONE RING *Wish* TWO WORLDS

Chapter 1

The bilious-green slime covering the wall's wooden boards ebbed with gruesome life; possessed of the ability to regenerate and multiply the substance of its horrid self despite the human's attempts to eradicate it. The foul sludge flaunted its everlasting power; mocking the inferior mortal standing helpless before its relentless supremacy.

Jennifer dipped the scrub brush in the sludgy water filling the bucket beside her feet and lifted the cleaning implement out again; observing the bits of emerald-colored goop wielding a merciless death grip on the tool's stiff bristles. "This is the job from hell," she muttered.

The roar of an approaching Porsche disrupted the post-dawn peace. It snapped off into silence and a solid thump indicated the closing of a car door. Scraping noises coming off the barn-aisle flooring suggested boot-clad feet attached to the shapely legs of Linda: a young blonde who had married well.

Jennifer forced a smile onto her face as she sped up the rate of her back-and-forth scrubbing strokes.

"You're not finished with that yet?"

The servant winced. "The spit smears all over instead of coming off and, well … I think hosing down the walls might be a better way to get rid of it."

"All these expensive shavings would get soaking wet." Linda removed her sunglasses and glared at her employee.

"I could sweep them into a pile in the middle of the stall."

"That won't work."

"I don't understand why your horses rub their mouths all over the walls after they eat the new alfalfa. They don't do that with the oat hay."

"That's not your concern." Linda let out a sigh that carried the scent of expensive whiskey to Jennifer's nostrils. "Do you know what time it is?"

Jennifer glanced at her watch. "Twenty minutes after seven."

"Did you groom Jack?"

"Yes."

"Tell you what … if you'll go to the feed store and pick up two bags of the morning pellets, I'll tack up Jack myself, and you can take a break from the scrubbing."

"Okay. Um … there's nothing left in the petty-cash box."

"Take care of the bill and I'll pay you back on Friday."

"I don't have any money."

"What?"

"I don't have any money. Well, I have enough to pay for groceries for the next couple of days, but after I buy food tonight, I'll be flat broke."

"Put it on a card."

"My credit card is maxed out."

"Don't you know how to handle money?"

"If I had any money, I might learn how to do that."

"Are you trying to get me to raise your salary?"

Jennifer turned her face away from the lady and stared out the open doorway at the back of the stall.

"I give you a nice place to live and four hundred a month. I don't see why you can't get by just fine on that."

"Yes, ma'am, but …"

"Are you going to complain about the trailer's broken heater again?"

"No."

"I'll go to the store myself! Have Jack tacked up when I get back."

"Yes, ma'am."

Jennifer squinted into the setting sun as she drove along the traffic-congested main street of the downtown area. Seeing something moving in the road, she slammed on the brakes. The paper bag in the front seat tipped over, dumping its load of groceries onto the rubber floor mat.

A tiny kitten, its white fur soiled with dirt, was darting to and fro between the moving cars. "No!" The woman turned on the emergency flashers and jumped out of the vehicle. Waving her arms, she attempted to alert the other rush-hour drivers to the situation, but they ignored her.

She ran onto the center divider of the four-lane road and stopped. The kitten was there; cowering next to a lamppost as it tried to decide where to bolt next.

"Kitty, kitty, kitty …" Horns began to blast as frustrated motorists attempted to get around Jennifer's car, which was blocking the left lane of traffic. "Kitty, kitty, kitty!"

The cat turned big blue eyes onto the woman's face and stepped towards her. She scooped the creature into her arms, returned to her car, set the feline on the floor, and drove off.

JENNIFER parked before a rusted 50-year-old trailer situated at a remote border of Linda's ranch. She looked down at the kitten crouching beside the pile of spilled groceries. "It's not much, kitty, but it's safer than the streets. When I turn on the oven and leave it open, it's warm in there; sort of. You'll like it."

She carried the cat inside the dwelling, set it on the bed, and returned to the car to retrieve the groceries. Opening the carton of eggs, she smiled. "Only one broken—great!" She stuffed the food items back into the bag and went inside the trailer.

"I don't have any meat, but I can give you some scrambled eggs. Maybe you can live on those until I get paid this Friday." The cat purred and rubbed its head against her outstretched hand. "Are you a boy or a girl? I don't know how to tell when you're so young."

There was the sound of a car driving up and parking. "Oh, crap! It's probably one of Linda's other lackeys telling me I need to take care of some mess or something. Maybe if I ignore them, they'll go away."

A knock on the flimsy metal door was followed by another. Jennifer groaned, hesitated, then went to respond to the visitor. As she opened the door, a silver Mercedes sped away; sending up a cloud of dust as it flew along the dirt road. There was a small package on the top step before her. She picked it up. "What's this?"

She closed the door before the approaching kitten could get out, sat on the threadbare sofa, and examined the package. "I don't know about this, kitty. There's no address or anything: it's just a box wrapped in brown paper. There could be something horrible in there." She set it on the floor. The cat gave the object a quick sniff and curled up next to it.

As she continued to regard the package, the growling Porsche drove up and parked by the trailer. A soft curse escaped her lips. "Why won't that woman leave me alone when I'm off duty?"

She grabbed the kitten and locked it in the tiny bedroom before opening the trailer door. Linda; an expression of irritation on her face; stood a few feet away from the bottom step of the entrance. "Who was that?"

"Who was what?"

"You know you're supposed to check with me before you allow anyone to visit you here."

"No one visited me."

"I just saw a Mercedes speeding out of here."

"I don't know who that was."

The blonde raised one eyebrow. "Are you sure?"

"Yes."

"All right." She started to turn away, then stopped. "When you do the midnight barn check, don't forget to give La Fleur her meds. The farrier will be here at seven tomorrow, so don't give Marquesa her morning feed until after he's done with her. There's a new bottle of the sedative in the barn fridge. Inject her with it fifteen minutes before the shoeing starts."

"I … yes, ma'am."

"You were going to say something else?"

'As long as you and your creepy vibes stay out of the barn, harpy, the poor horse won't need a sedative!' Not the best words to fling at one's boss, so Jennifer held back. "I wasn't going to say anything." She looked down at her work boots.

"Have a nice evening." The blonde departed.

Jennifer released the kitten from the bedroom and returned to the couch. "Shall I open the box, kitty? I don't know … just looking at it makes me feel weird."

The cat rubbed its cheek against a corner of the package and purred.

"Well, since you're not scared, it must be all right." She picked it up. "Maybe I should fix you some eggs first." She looked at the cat, then at the box. "My curiosity is killing me: I gotta open it."

She peeled off the brown paper; revealing a white cardboard box. Lifting its lid, she discovered another box; this one covered in black velvet. "It looks like a ring box." She picked it up and saw a piece of folded paper in the bottom of the white box. "A note, maybe?"

The unfolded paper revealed a paragraph handwritten in black ink: *"The enclosed ring will give you five wishes. Put it on your finger, say 'This is what I wish for,' state your wish, and finish by saying 'That is my wish.' Be careful."*

"What?" Jennifer leaned against the backrest of the sofa. "Somebody has a perverse sense of humor for sure!"

Opening the velvet box, she withdrew a plain gold band. "Oh, it's heavy. I could sell it to a jewelry store and get enough cash to buy lots of cat food for you." She slipped it onto the ring finger of her left hand. Her brown eyes opened wide, and she sucked in a deep gulp of air.

The gold band had a heartbeat.

She pulled the ring off, jammed it back into its box, and set it on the floor.

JENNIFER sat on the couch for half an hour staring at the box. When her stomach started growling, she remembered she hadn't fed the cat. "Hang on, sweetie. I'll fix you something."

She scrambled three eggs and served a small pile to the kitten, whose focused gulping indicated a state of starvation. "I'm so sorry, baby. I won't let you go hungry again."

Seated on the couch, she scarfed down her eggs, set the plate on the sofa cushion beside her, and went back to staring at the box.

HALF AN hour later, she rose and went into the part of the trailer that passed for a kitchen. She put the dirty dishes in the sink, pulled open a drawer, and removed a pad of paper and a pen.

Returning to the couch, she patted the cushion beside her. "Come here, kitty!" The cat curled up next to her and began to groom itself as she turned her attention to the writing pad.

"I read 'The Monkey's Paw,' kitty. I'm not going to screw this up and cause innocent people to suffer so I can get what I want." She began to write down her first wish; pausing occasionally to consider all aspects and possibilities of certain conditions.

After several minutes, she put the pen aside. "Here goes nothing, cat. I … I shouldn't take such a risk, but I gotta tell ya: this job is killing me. A couple of months ago, one of Linda's horses freaked out and knocked me down while I was leading her. She was trying to run away from something that spooked her and my body was in her way, so I got hurt. When I told boss lady about it, all she said was, 'Did anyone else see it happen?' Why did she even say that? Then she got mad because I had to take a week off work to recover from the concussion! And that's just the tip of the huge mass of frozen chunks of crap that constitute this awful job, baby cat. I want to have the power to live a good, safe life and never ever again have to say, 'Yes, ma'am,' to someone I don't respect."

She put the ring on her finger; fighting to remain calm as it began to throb with that terrifying heartbeat. Taking a deep breath, she read aloud the words on the writing pad:

"This is what I wish for: 50 billion dollars deposited immediately, as in right now, into my present checking account; money for which federal and state taxes have already been paid, and 10 million dollars in cash to be waiting for me on my bed when I get back from today's midnight barn check. If this money cannot be materialized out of thin air, take it from criminals and/or people who run companies that use slave labor. No one shall die as a result of this money being provided to me. Nothing bad will happen at all, except maybe the nasty people whose money has been transferred to me will be sad. The nasty people will not know that I have their money and no one in the government will get after me about why I suddenly have all this money. The money provided to me shall without exception be legal tender; no counterfeit bills or bills bearing serial numbers that will flag them as being from a criminal source or a bank robbery or anything illegal. That is my wish."

She put the ring back into its box and settled down on the couch for a nap; the kitten curled up on her shoulder.

Jennifer left her car and approached the trailer. It was a near-freezing night; causing her to put the heaviest blankets on all of Linda's eight horses. As she walked up the steps to her front door, she pulled her knit cap down over her ears and forehead; pushing her long black hair away from her face.

She entered the trailer, switched on a lamp, made for the oven, and turned it on to the highest setting. As she opened the door to let the heat fill the front of the small dwelling, she spotted the sleeping cat on the sofa. The creature had groomed itself quite effectively: its coat now pure white.

"I have to figure out what gender you are so I can name you," she whispered.

She looked at the closed bedroom door; afraid to open it and meet with certain disappointment. 'It was pretty silly of me to believe I could make a wish and have it granted,' she thought. 'I'm just so miserable, and I need a miracle to get me out of this awful hopeless place.'

Standing before the oven to soak up the heat, she pulled off her cap and knit gloves. A minute later, she removed her bulky jacket.

'Guess I ought to open up the bedroom to let the heat in.' She went to that door and opened it. Seeing something unusual in the darkness, she switched on the bedroom light.

Tall stacks of loose bills piled up to the low ceiling of the chamber covered the twin-sized mattress and bedroom floor: evidence of Jennifer's failure to specify large denominations only when she made her wish.

Her bony posterior hit the linoleum flooring hard, though she didn't feel the pain of it. A choking sound trying to escape from her throat roused the kitten, who trotted over to sit beside the woman gazing at the mountains of money.

A few minutes later, she was able to speak. "I think we got some power now, kitty." She rose and went to the sofa, picked up the pad of paper and a pen, and began to write out a plan:

1st thing: buy cat food, litter and a litter box, and a reliable car. And some expensive ice cream. Chocolate mint would be good.

2nd thing: get a house impervious to home-invasion robberies. With central heating. ~~And a dishwasher.~~ I can wash dishes myself.

3rd thing: buy a bed and a comfy chair. And a vacuum cleaner. And a computer that doesn't freeze up and crash every two minutes. And a table for sitting and eating at, and lots of books. Have them delivered to impervious house. Buy lamps - I don't own any lamps. And sheets, blankets, towels, and a toilet plunger. Nothing worse than not having a toilet plunger when you really need one.

4th thing: give Linda notice.

5th thing: get out of here.

"You and I are sleeping on the couch tonight, kitty." She closed the bedroom door so the oven's heat wouldn't be wasted on that space and settled down on the sofa.

Continuing to work at the stable without mentioning her windfall to anyone was a challenge, but if Linda heard about it, she would surely have one of her temper tantrums and throw Jennifer off the property before she had acquired a landlord-free home. It might be hard to find a hotel that accepted cats, so it was best to wait until permanent accommodations were acquired and the keys were in the novice billionaire's possession. The boss lady did start to conduct an intensive interrogation regarding why her servant was driving an expensive new car, but the response 'It's personal' brought an end to the inquiries.

On the day the necessary furnishings were delivered to her new home, Jennifer drove up the hill to Linda's mansion and rang the bell at the front door. The housekeeper admitted the visitor into the grand foyer and went to look for her mistress.

Linda appeared a few minutes later. "I was in my theatre watching a film. What do you want?"

"Most people would simply say, 'I was watching a movie,' but you just had to mention that you were in your special little private theatre. Why is that?" The blonde's mouth opened. "I don't really need an answer to that, Linda. I know exactly why you said it." Jennifer smiled. "I'm here to give my notice. I'll allow you a week to find my replacement before I leave."

"You won't allow me anything! Get off my property!"

"I'm saying this for the very last time: yes, ma'am."

Jennifer felt a foreign thrill race through her body as she descended the marble steps. 'I better not allow myself to enjoy power too much,' she thought. 'I don't want to turn into the boss lady and end up having whiskey for breakfast every morning.'

She got into her car and looked at the mansion. "That palace is a very sad place." She started the engine and drove away.

JENNIFER pulled her fingers out of the wire grill covering the side opening of the cat carrier. Having contact with her hand soothed the kitten during the car ride, but now the entrance to the enclosed neighborhood had to be handled.

It didn't take long to deal with the armed guard at the gatehouse. Though he didn't yet recognize her at first sight, the man was polite and cordial, and he made her feel safe.

She looked at the big homes set far back from the main street as she drove towards her house. Not once did she see a human. "I guess they all hang out in their backyards when they want to be outside. Still … it feels kind of like an expensive, well-kept ghost town. We'll just have to get used to it; right, kitty?"

A one-lane road led up a hill to a home situated on a two-acre lot: the largest house in this exclusive community. She pulled into the driveway, heading for the detached garage, but something made her stop.

It was a cold, twisting feeling in her gut: something wasn't quite right. She took her hands off the steering wheel and dropped them into her lap. Staring at the front of her oversized mansion, she shook her head slowly back and forth. "I don't know about this, kitty. I don't know … something's wrong."

She put the car into park—the engine still running—and looked around at the gardens and trees. "I cannot imagine what could be wrong: the security in this place borders on overkill. There can't be any criminals skulking about. Why do I feel afraid to get out of my car?"

Taking a deep breath, she put the car into drive. "It must be 'cause it's getting dark. I've never been here at night before. A big empty house in the dark is always spooky." Glancing at the cat, she smiled. "Thanks for being such a good listener. If I didn't have you, I'd be talking to myself all the time."

She dug around in her glove box, found the remote for the garage door, and pressed the button. It was gratifying to see the wooden panels slide up into invisibility at her command, and she giggled. "That's so cool."

Anticipating the warmth of programmed central heating that had kicked in prior to her arrival, she pushed aside her anxiety. As she carried the cat and a suitcase along the stone-paved walkway to a side door of the house, the prospect of a night spent in luxurious comfort blotted out all lingering doubts. "Heat, a proper bathtub, a big bed with new sheets and blankets, and nobody knocking on my door at weird hours telling me I have to hop to it and perform whatever chore her ladyship desires. I can sleep as late as I want. Yeah!"

She unlocked the door, entered the kitchen, and pressed a switch on the wall. Shining chrome and stainless-steel surfaces reflected light beaming down from an array of recessed lamps set in the ceiling. The wrought-iron pot rack suspended over the central island looked a little sad, with only one copper pot dangling there all alone, but the visual elegance of the marble countertops and polished-granite floor tiles made up for the scarcity of Jennifer's culinary supplies.

Setting the carrier down, she opened its door and released the kitten, who had been declared a male and then neutered by the vet who tended to the little creature's health needs. "Boris—go explore!"

He sniffed the floor tiles for a moment or two, then sprang into a gallop that carried him out of the kitchen and into parts unknown. Jennifer went back to her car and retrieved her purse and a paper sack containing fast food. Returning to the kitchen, she paused at an electronic panel set beside the door and turned on the security system before settling in for the night.

THE WOMAN and cat slept soundly in the new bed; unaware of the female figure that stood in the center of the room. The lady was of gigantic proportions; her head almost touching the high ceiling. Two thick braids of platinum-blonde hair fell below her waist, which was encircled by a belt of twisted golden cables cinching a loose white gown that fell to the floor in luxurious folds of heavy fabric. Her bare arms were adorned by wide bracelets of yellow metal embossed with stylized animal figures, and upon one shoulder perched a raven. Beside her bare feet, a huge black wolf stood at attention.

She smiled at the sleeping figure. "Lucky lady."

The cat woke at the sound of her voice and jumped to his feet. Jennifer opened her eyes, and her lower jaw dropped. "What? What? What?"

"You might think about improving your conversational skills."

"What?"

The woman and her creatures vanished.

Jennifer shook her head. "I guess eating chili fries right before bed was a bad idea." She picked up the kitten. Pressing him to her chest, she went back to sleep.

CHAPTER 2

Jennifer sat in her dining room. Before her, a plastic jug of milk stood beside a jelly doughnut. Three layers of paper towels served as a placemat; protecting the plastic surface of the portable card table.

She took the top off the jug and swallowed a big gulp of the ice-cold liquid. A bite of the doughnut revealed that the day-old pastry was stale, but it was the only food in the house other than cat kibble, so its consumption was necessary.

The woman leaned back in her folding chair and looked to one side, where a wall of picture windows and glass doors showed a view of a patio. A flight of stairs leading down from the far side of the pavement led to a swimming pool, though it wasn't visible from inside the ground floor of the house.

She addressed the cat who lay on the floor beside her chair. "I gotta get rid of that pool, Boris. I don't like swimming in pools. It's almost as bad as riding horses in an arena; going round and round in circles with walls all around you. Anyway … it's a waste of water and something of a hazard. Maybe I can fill it with dirt and start a vegetable garden. I could make holes in the bottom with a jackhammer so water can drain out. But I might not be strong enough to handle a jackhammer, and I'd have to put in a million cubic feet of dirt, too." She paused. "Ah! I have money! I can pay someone else to do it." She smiled.

A shrill ringing made her gasp in alarm. "Oh, that's terrible! I gotta get a different bell."

She rose and went to the front door. A short, stout woman in a pale-blue cotton dress stood on the flagstones before the entrance. Her curly black hair was twisted into a tight bun at the back of her neck, and she appeared to be in her mid-thirties. She held a plastic container and offered it to Jennifer.

"What … hi. That's for me?"

"Mrs. Collier wants you to have this lasagne. I made it myself." The woman smiled.

"Who is Mrs. Collier?"

"Your neighbor on the left."

"Okay. Thank you so much! I really appreciate it." Jennifer accepted the gift. "I don't have anything to eat except a stale doughnut."

"There's enough lasagne in there for eight people."

"It'll last me for several meals, then. I'm all alone here, except for a cat."

"Just you alone in this big house?"

"It was the only place available for sale that I could get into quickly. I was in a rush to find a new home."

"You'll like this neighborhood. It's very safe and quiet."

"You referred to my neighbor as 'Mrs.' You work for her?"

"Yes, I'm the cook."

"Since you're a pro, I'm betting this lasagne will be great!"

The woman smiled and nodded.

"I should get to the store. I don't have any plates or silverware or anything. I don't wanna eat lasagne with my hands."

"You were in a rush to move in, weren't you?"

"Yup. At the place I was living before I came here, everything in the, uh, house except my clothes belonged to my boss, so I don't own anything much." She paused. "I do own a real nice copper pot. I guess I should've bought more practical stuff when I was in that department store, but ... I didn't."

"I see." The visitor nodded. "I'll be on my way. If you need anything at all, just go around to the back entrance of the Collier home. I'll be happy to help you."

"Thanks again. I really appreciate the gesture."

"Bye." The woman turned and walked away.

Jennifer closed the door. 'My neighbor sent her servant to greet me,' she thought. 'Maybe she's too shy to come herself.' Walking towards the kitchen, she realized she hadn't exchanged names with the cook. 'I gotta work on my etiquette, I guess.'

She put the lasagna in the fridge and picked up her purse from the kitchen's island. "Boris!"

The training had worked: he came at the call of his name. Bending down, the woman stroked his head and looked into his eyes. “I’m going to the store to buy lots of stuff, okay? Don’t be afraid of being left alone. If you see any blonde giants, well; I don’t know what to tell you about that. It was just a bad dream, anyway.” She stood upright. “Compared to my usual nightmares, that one was pretty mild.”

As she approached the garage, she turned to look back. Boris stood on the sill of a kitchen window watching her. She waved. “Bye, baby!”

TWO DAYS later, the lasagne was gone. Jennifer, bewildered by her high-tech dishwasher’s overabundance of choices in settings and functions, scrubbed the plastic container in the sink along with the other dirty dishes.

Walking along the driveway of the Collier home, she glanced at the front of the mansion. Employing furtive, darting looks in an attempt to not look overly inquisitive, she observed a face peeking out from between the curtains of a top-floor window. It was impossible to tell if it was male or female; young or old; due to the reflection of the morning sun on the glass. The only features visible were two dark eyes in a pale face that disappeared as the curtains closed.

She went around the back of the house and saw a door whose modest appearance implied ‘servant’s entrance.’ As she hesitated a few feet away, the door opened. “Miss Grace!” The cook smiled.

“How do you know my name?”

"Online research."

"I see." She nodded. "Please call me Jennifer. What's your …"

"Ophelia."

"I'm delighted to make your acquaintance, Ophelia." She handed the food container to the cook. "Thanks again. That was the best food I've eaten in a long time."

"Don't you want to know what else I learned about you?"

"I'm afraid to ask."

"You're the seventh richest person in the world and no one can identify your source of income."

Jennifer laughed. "Uh, huh."

Ophelia grinned. "You're not a criminal, are you?"

"I don't think a lone criminal can earn that much money. I mean; they can get rich, but …"

"I believe the previous owner of the house you just bought was a criminal."

"Really?"

"He lost his fortune overnight. That makes me think he had dirty dealings."

"Overnight?" Jennifer's body stiffened.

"We heard some awful yelling coming from the house one day. A few hours later, an ambulance went wailing up the driveway. It seems the man committed suicide."

"Someone killed themselves in my house? The realtor didn't mention that."

"His housekeeper found him lying on the floor; alive but unconscious. She told me he died in the ambulance on the way to the hospital, so I guess you don't have to worry about ghosts in your home."

"When did all that happen?"

"It was my brother's birthday: January 12th."

"This year?"

"Yes."

Jennifer grabbed onto the edge of the countertop near her. "Thanks again for the lasagne. I have to … I have things to do at home."

"Okay. Drop by any time!"

"I'll do that, Ophelia."

Back at home, she lay on her bed staring at the ceiling. January 12th was the day she made her wish.

Boris hopped up onto the bed and rubbed his head against Jennifer's arm. It had been an hour since her departure from the Collier home and she was finally starting to feel better, though certainly not good.

She sat up and stared out the window. The view showed a fountain set in the center of the big lawn stretching out across the property on the right side of the house.

"That thing is tacky," she told the cat. "This whole huge house is tacky. It's nothing but a big ugly McMansion. I can afford to dump this place and buy a home that isn't a vulgar display of tasteless wealth.

Yeah; I'll find something better and get out of here!" She put her feet on the floor and started to stand up.

"How are you today, Miss Grace?" The blonde giantess had materialized in the center of the room and stood looking down at the dark-haired lady.

"What the …"

"Ah, you've expanded your vocabulary: you used two words!"

Jennifer fell back onto the bed and collapsed. Boris ran to the foot of the mattress and stood staring at the black wolf; his fluffy tail twitching. The raven extended a wing in a stretching movement, and the cat switched his gaze onto it; crouching down into a predatory position.

"Careful, small cat. This bird can tear you apart in two bites."

Boris spun about, ran to Jennifer's side, and tried to hide his head under her sweater.

"Don't you have anything to say, Miss Grace?"

Jennifer whimpered.

"I'll give you time to compose yourself." The giantess began to shrink, as did her oversized animals. When they reached the size of ordinary creatures, the woman took a seat in a club chair near the window.

'I'm not going to faint,' Jennifer thought. 'I just spent two years in a job where I had to summon up raw courage out of nowhere every single day in order to intimidate half-wild horses who regarded me as an amusing chew-toy. I had no one to keep my spirits up as I lived under the thumb of an emotionally abusive boss, and I survived. I am tough … I am strong!' She clenched her hands into fists. 'I'll treat this lady just like that psycho thoroughbred who used to charge at me in the pasture.' She sat up. "Who the hell are you?"

"Nice!" the lady said. "You can go far in this world with a threatening voice like that."

"You didn't answer my question!" She rose to her feet and took a step towards the woman. The wolf growled and so did Jennifer; baring her teeth at the canine.

The visitor laughed. "You're overcompensating for your fear. If you keep it up, Fenright will not respond well. One shouldn't attempt to dominate a wolf when one doesn't know what one is doing."

Jennifer took a step back and sat on the bed. "Kindly identify yourself."

"My name is Marit."

"What are you?"

"You can think of me as an angel if you like."

"Can I think of you as a frog if I like?"

"Yes, though I can't imagine why you would want to do that."

"You don't want to tell me what you really are."

Marit smiled. "I am connected to the power of the ring, and I'm here to keep an eye on your activities: that's all you need to know."

"I think I need to know a lot more than that."

"You need to know nothing more than what I've told you."

"I disagree."

The woman smiled and stroked the wolf's head. "I'm curious about something, Miss Grace."

"As am I."

"Why did you wish for 50 billion dollars? Most people wish for millions. Why billions?"

"Real estate in this part of California is very expensive."

"Please …"

"All right. I … I want to feel safe. I want to be able to have absolute control over my environment for the rest of my life. I've heard stories about lottery winners who go through their millions in a couple of years and end up with nothing, so I know millions can't last for a lifetime. I never want to have nothing again. When I had nothing, I was … I, uh … I was hurt by violent criminals. I want to be safe."

"Considering that, it makes sense that you'd wish for unlimited wealth in an attempt to ensure no more traumas in your life."

"I would've liked that statement a lot more if you hadn't said 'attempt.' Are you trying to make me feel insecure?"

"No, I'm sorry." Marit bowed her head for a moment. "Tell me, please … how do you feel about the man who committed suicide in this house?"

"He didn't die in here, though that doesn't matter. I feel terrible. I didn't want anyone to get hurt. I was very specific about that when I made my wish. My money would come from criminals, but none of them would die."

"The man was heartless and cruel. He built his fortune on the suffering of others and deserved to lose it."

"There must have been some bit of heart in him. Truly cruel people don't usually commit suicide, I think."

"Sometimes they do. People can be unpredictable."

"Yes." Jennifer nodded. "Who put the ring outside my door?"

"Ryan. He was in the car behind you when you stopped to rescue the cat. He'd been searching for months for a person to pass it on to and wasn't finding anyone he could trust. When you went after the cat, he saw it as proof that you have a good heart. He too wished for a fortune and saw people became fake around him in hopes of getting a piece of that wealth for themselves; pretending to be good-hearted when they were not."

"Were you in his car with him when I rescued the cat?"

"No, he told me about it after he gave you the ring."

"How do you know what I wished for, and how did you learn about the dead man?"

"As I said before, I am connected to the power of the ring."

"That tells me nothing." Jennifer shifted her position on the bed; sitting cross-legged. "With all the power the ring wields, I would think that someone would've used it to make the world a paradise. It's gone through the hands of quite a few people, hasn't it?"

"No … don't even think about it."

"Why?"

"Consider the unexpected consequence of your first wish. If you use the ring's power to change the entire world, one tiny mistake could cause utter chaos. You already killed one person; don't risk destroying the lives of countless people!"

"That wasn't supposed to happen!"

"There's only one way to free yourself of your burden of guilt: wish to have the money returned and make everything go back to the way it was."

"The idea of going back into poverty … I can't do that. I know Linda was working up to firing me. She made a list of everything she didn't like about me—I saw it in her office. She would've thrown me out onto the street with no notice and no severance pay, and I would've had to go back to living in my car. I'd rather be dead than homeless again."

"If you were to return the money, you'd be putting some truly nasty people back into business."

"Like I said, I can't even consider that option." The raven left the woman's shoulder and flew to the bed. Landing near Jennifer, he stared at the kitten sitting beside her. "If you hurt my cat, there will be trouble for you, bird!"

"He's just curious. Don't worry about him."

Jennifer eyeballed the raven. "He's huge; like some kind of big black predatory goose."

"Do you keep the ring in a secure location?"

"What? Oh, um, I put it in a safe-deposit box at my bank."

Marit nodded and beckoned to the bird. He returned to her shoulder, and she rose to her feet. "I have certain matters I must attend to. It was a pleasure meeting you, Miss Grace."

"Yeah."

Putting one hand atop the wolf's head, the woman smiled and disappeared. It wasn't a dramatic exit accompanied by fancy special effects: Marit and her animals simply stopped being there.

Jennifer gasped for air, then rubbed her face with both hands. "Boris, I'm not enjoying this. I don't know if that woman was a teleporting alien or a spirit or a hallucination or what!"

Falling back, she lay on the bed for half an hour; letting out stress-inspired sighs and occasional groans. Finally abandoning what was surely pointless contemplation, she sat up. 'If I keep lying around thinking about stuff I can't understand, I'll go nuts. I need a brain wipe.' Picking up the kitten, she rose to her feet. "Let's go downstairs and play with my new computer. Maybe I can find funny cat videos to entertain us."

Chapter 3

Jennifer looked down at the backyard from an upstairs window. Outside, men armed with heavy machinery were dismantling the swimming pool and making a great deal of noise.

She turned to the ever-present white beast at her feet. "It's a big mess right now, Boris, but in time there'll be a circulating filtered creek and a pond so wild critters can drink and bathe. We'll even have a small waterfall. It'll be nice!"

The cat rubbed against her ankle. "You know … every time I leave this house, I feel bad about leaving you all alone. I think I'll go to the animal shelter and get you a friend. Yeah; an old female who'll be your mommy. Problem is I'll want to bring everyone in the shelter home with me so they don't get killed." She tightened the elastic band holding her ponytail in place as she considered the dilemma. "I know—I'll give the shelter a bunch of money so they can build a big comfortable facility and make them promise to stop, uh … eliminating animals."

She sighed. "I don't know anything about giving away money to organizations. I bet it's way more complicated than I'd like it to be. I mean; giving them the money would be easy enough, but how do I make sure they do the right thing with it?

"I guess I should talk to an actual human being instead of a cat. I'll go next door and see if Mrs. Collier knows more about being rich than I do."

JENNIFER was halfway up the Collier driveway when an automatic-sprinkler system erupted into action; sending out hissing sprays of water that caused the startled woman to curse. Errant mist floating on the morning breeze dampened her cheek, and she wiped it off with one hand.

She stopped a few feet away from the house's front entrance. 'The lady sent a servant to welcome me to the neighborhood instead of coming herself,' she thought. 'I could be asking for a world of hurt if I ring that doorbell.' Turning away, she started to walk to the back of the dwelling.

The sound of the front door opening caused her to pause. A man stood in the entryway. "Can I help you?" He was a dark-haired fellow who appeared to be around Jennifer's age; in his early thirties, perhaps.

She approached the man. "I live next door. I, uh, want to ask Mrs. Collier a question about … something."

"My mother is upstairs reading. I'll fetch her for you. Please," he waved a hand towards the interior of the house, "come in."

"Thank you."

Jennifer followed the man across the polished marble flooring of the foyer and down some steps to a large living area. He indicated that she should take a seat on a sofa and departed.

An older woman soon appeared. Tall and thin, she had steel-gray hair twisted into a chignon. Her skin was exceptionally white, and her rather large brown eyes betrayed a slight level of fatigue.

"Good morning, Miss Grace."

"Good morning, Mrs. Collier." Jennifer offered her hand to the lady, who shook it. The older woman's hand was cold and stiff. "How do you know my name?"

"Ophelia told us."

"Oh."

"My son said you have a question for me." The lady remained standing as she looked into Jennifer's eyes.

"I, uh … I have no experience with charitable giving, and I thought you might know something about it. I want to make a large donation to the local animal shelter with the stipulation that they will stop, uh, putting down unwanted dogs and cats."

"There's no need for that stipulation. Our shelter is a no-kill facility."

"Oh!" Jennifer blushed. "I'm so sorry I bothered you. I didn't even think to check on that; I just assumed …" She shook her head. "I'm so sorry!"

"There's no need to apologize." Mrs. Collier took a step back. "Is there anything else?"

"No, no." She rose from the couch. "I'm sorry. I'll go now."

She bolted; making for the front door in a fast walk bordering on a gallop. "Nice meeting you!" she called out as she escaped through the entrance.

As she jogged towards the driveway, the man came around the corner of the house. "Miss Grace!"

With the greatest reluctance, she stopped. "Yes?"

"My mother is going through some rough times. If she appeared less than gracious, I apologize."

"She was fine. I just, um … I'm not very good with people. Animals, yeah; people, no! And aliens—I'm real good with aliens!" She put her hands before her stomach and clasped them together in a tight squeeze. Tears were forming in her eyes.

"Are you referring to immigrants?"

"No, no, no!" She began to weep.

"What's wrong?"

"I … I really need someone to talk to. I don't have any family or friends and I need to talk to someone!"

"I'm not busy right now. Do you want to talk to me?"

"You're sure you're not busy?"

"I'm sure."

"Can you come to my house?"

"That would be fine."

Jennifer wiped her eyes. "Come on, then."

When they entered her house, the man stopped. "By the way; my name's Brett."

"I'm Jennifer."

He looked over the unfurnished living area. "You haven't finished moving in yet?"

"No, I'm finished. I just don't own much furniture. I should probably buy a couch or two, but I haven't gotten around to it."

"I suppose there's no rush." Brett smiled.

"Nope; no rush. I have furniture in the rooms I use, so … I'm comfortable."

"If you happy and comfortable, I see no reason to change anything."

"I can't say that I'm happy." Jennifer pointed to the entrance of a corridor. "Let's go into my office so we can sit down."

Once in that room, they settled into comfortable chairs. The woman took a deep breath. "I don't know where to start."

"Take your time."

She stared at the floor. "I have a ring that grants wishes. That's how I got the money to buy this house. I was really poor and then I was a billionaire in a matter of minutes. Maybe less than minutes; I think the money went into my bank account as soon as I made my wish."

"Really?"

"If it weren't in a safe-deposit box, I could show the ring to you. It has a pulsing heart beat."

Brett blinked and shifted his gaze to the window. "Who's making all that noise out there?"

"I'm getting rid of the pool."

He nodded and continued to stare out the window.

"You don't believe me, of course."

He nodded again.

"I'll show you my checking account so you can see for yourself." She went to her desk and turned on the computer. When the display came to life, she signed in at her bank's site and went to the online statements. "Look at this."

Brett sighed and went to her side.

"You see how much I have now. Let me go back a bit to when all that money landed in there." She scrolled down to the huge deposit. "You see that? I had two dollars in my account, and then I had 50 billion. When I scroll down further you can see how, for the past year, that account never had much more than four hundred dollars in it, and at the end of every month, it was either almost empty or totally empty. Look at the past year."

Brett sat before the computer and looked at the statements. He went through the year of poverty, glancing at the purchases and payments listed, then returned to the huge deposit. "The source listed for the transaction is a cash deposit."

"Do you think there's any reasonable way I could've gotten my hands on that much cash? No lottery would pay out that much money, and even if it did, it wouldn't be paid in cash."

"I can't think of a reasonable way for you to get that money, but since magic rings don't exist, your explanation doesn't work for me. Maybe you had the money all your life and it was kept in another account somewhere, and you took it all out and put it into this account."

"I carried 50 billion dollars into my bank and told the teller to deposit it? That's ridiculous. A magic ring's the only explanation, so you ought to accept it."

"Maybe you should wish for me to believe you."

"I only get five wishes. Your approval of my most certainly true story isn't important enough for me to waste one of them."

The man raised his eyebrows. "I see your point about not being good with people."

"Uh, huh."

"Now you've made me curious about how you acquired your fortune. I'm going to have do some digging."

"Go for it! You won't find anything."

Brett leaned back into the flexible desk chair until it was close to tipping over backwards. "Where do aliens enter into all this?"

"What?"

"You said you're good with aliens."

"Oh, that. Never mind. It was just temporary insanity."

"You're sure it was temporary?"

Jennifer shook her head. "I should stick with just talking to my cat."

"You talk to your cat?"

"He doesn't lack imagination."

Brett grinned and rose from the chair. "I'll be on my way. I promise you: I will find out where your money comes from."

"*Bonne chance*, dude."

Jennifer set the cardboard cat carrier on the kitchen floor. Bowing down, she spoke to the feline contained within it. "Don't get mad, lady. I'll let you and Boris get acquainted for a few minutes before I let you out." She stood upright. "Boris!"

He trotted into the kitchen; immediately realizing there was a strange creature in the container. As he drew near, a dreadful hissing emanated from the box. Boris froze, but his curiosity got the best of him and he began to sniff at the ventilation holes in the carrier. Jennifer could heard the confined cat's claws scratching at the holes.

"I don't know if she's scratching because she wants to get out or because she hates you. Oh, dear." The woman paused to think for a moment. "I think she's stressed and wants to get out. Maybe galloping through the house will relax her." She released the brown tabby, who flew out of sight with the kitten close behind. "Show her where the litter boxes are, Boris!"

As Jennifer climbed the stairs, she smiled; remembering the look on the shelter employee's face when she handed her a check for enough money to build a second wing for the establishment. 'There are bright sides to this situation,' she thought.

She went into her bedroom, intending to switch her jeans and sweater for comfortable sweats. As she headed for a bureau, a voice spoke behind her. "Good afternoon, Miss Grace."

She spun around to see the blonde and her creatures. "Crap!"

"You're not happy about my visit, I assume."

"You're right about that! Would you please leave me alone? How am I supposed to maintain my sanity with you popping in and out of here? Go away, you freaking alien!"

"Alien?"

"You're not of this world, and that's the truth. Get lost!"

"I am the power behind the ring. I gave you a fortune, and you show no gratitude."

"You said you're connected to the power of the ring, but you haven't proved that. I don't know who or what you are, and I don't want you appearing and disappearing in my house. Get out!"

"Very well." Marit disappeared.

Jennifer collapsed onto the floor. "I can't handle this." She lowered her head, then raised it again. "I can handle this!"

The piercing sound of the doorbell blasted through the house, and she cursed. "I gotta get that awful thing replaced."

She stomped down the stairs and went to the door. Opening it, she saw Marit standing there.

"You apparently didn't understand what I was trying to express earlier. Why have you come back?"

"I thought if I came to your door like a mortal human, it would make you more comfortable."

"It does not make me more comfortable."

"I think this is a bad time for you. I'll try again later." Marit vanished.

Jennifer slammed the door and went into the kitchen. Digging through her tool drawer, she found a screwdriver, returned to her front entrance, and went outside.

She glared at the golden plaque framing the button for the doorbell. "I'll put a stop to you," she muttered.

As she began to loosen one of the screws holding the button assembly in place, she heard the sound of approaching footsteps. Turning, she saw Brett standing a few feet away.

"You look confused. What's wrong?"

He shook his head back and forth. "I think I've lost my mind."

"Okay." She paused for a moment. "Do you want to talk about it?"

"I, uh …" He took a deep breath. "This is embarrassing."

"Come on, guy—spit it out."

"I'm hallucinating."

"Really? What did you see?"

"I was walking up the drive here and I saw a lady at your door. She was wearing a long white dress. There was a big black bird on her shoulder, I think, and a large black dog beside her. She was standing at your door and then she was gone; just gone."

"That was Marit."

"I don't feel so good."

"Come inside and collapse. I collapse all the time: it's nothing to be ashamed of."

"I don't think I can move."

"Come on." She stuffed the screwdriver into the waistband of her jeans, went to his side, and put her arm around his shoulders. "I'll help you."

Walking slowly, they made their way to Jennifer's office. She helped him into a chair and took a seat opposite him.

"Can I get you anything; a glass of water, maybe?"

"No, thanks."

A streak of brown fur flew past the open door, followed by a tiny white blur. Brett's head jerked back, and his eyes opened wide.

"Not to worry: I just got a new cat who's getting used to the house." She leaned forward. "Why were you coming up my driveway?"

"I wanted to tell you something. I don't recall … oh, yes: I remember now. You were right about the lack of information regarding the source of your money. All my sources could learn about you is that you were born and raised in California and worked a series of low-paying jobs since leaving high school. You were married for three years, and your ex-husband moved to Alabama after the divorce. He's never risen above a working-class income and neither did your parents, who are deceased. There's no evidence of any relatives who might've left you a large inheritance."

"That's right. It's been a pretty unremarkable life up to now: nothing but a boring struggle to survive." Jennifer smiled. "Are you feeling better yet?"

"Not exactly."

"I know the feeling. I don't know who or what Marit is, but she tends to come and go in an unorthodox manner. I hate that."

"You don't know who she is?"

"She showed up for the first time a few days ago; maybe a week or so ago? I don't remember exactly. Anyway, she appeared in my bedroom and told me a bunch of stuff I don't really believe. I mean … I believe some of it, but she was evasive when I asked her what she is."

"You carried on a conversation with someone who just appeared in your bedroom? I think I'd pass out."

Jennifer looked down at the floor. "I've had experience with handling shocking situations and developed a knack for falling apart only after the immediate crisis is over. If I concentrate real hard and remind myself that I'm strong, I do okay."

Brett ran a hand through his hair and sighed. "I'm beginning to suspect that your ring is for real."

"It is, and I'd appreciate it if you wouldn't share that suspicion with anyone. Have you told anybody what I told you?"

"No. I thought you were crazy, and it would be unkind to go around telling people that my neighbor is nuts."

"Thank you. If word got out; whoa! That would be bad. Can you imagine all the crazies that would be trying to find a way to get their hands on it?"

"This is shattering my view of reality."

"Just go back to life as it was. Keep on living like nothing happened. Reality hasn't changed; it just has a couple of wrinkles you didn't know about." Jennifer chuckled. "In a few days, you'll forget all about this."

"You think so?"

"Let's go outside and look at the big hole where the pool used to be. I can show you the plans for the new garden and water elements."

"That sounds like a good distraction."

MARIT STOOD very still, hidden in the trees at the back of Jennifer's property. As she watched the couple looking into the great hole in the ground, her hands clenched into fists.

Fenright was beside her. No longer camouflaged by the image of a wolf; he showed his true state as a small half-simian; half-human creature. "When, dear lady; when will it be time?"

"I often think it will never be time." Marit patted the head of the minion crouching by her feet. "We must not, however, lose our patience and make a foolish move."

The tiny winged serpent on her shoulder spread his wings and drifted down onto the ground. "I say we attack!" he croaked.

"Don't be silly, Verny. The ring is locked in a safe too small for me to enter, so I must use artifice to obtain it." The lady relaxed her hands and stretched out her fingers. "I've been careless in my dealings with the woman. I need to rethink my strategy."

A large form flew into view and landed atop one of the chimneys of the mansion. Seeing the creature, Marit hissed. "What is Baldrick doing here? Which one of you told him about the ring?"

Verny pressed his wings tight against his serpentine form and shook his head. "Not me—I would never do such a thing!"

"I would die before I would betray you, dearest lady!" Fenright clasped his hands before him and bowed down on one knee. "I swear that to be true!"

Marit looked at her creatures. "I know both of you are terrible liars, so I will accept that you are telling the truth." She turned her gaze back to the tall form atop the chimney. "If he doesn't learn to conceal himself properly, one of the locals will blast him to pieces with a firearm. No subtlety in that boy; none at all." She smiled. "That will be his downfall."

"You could set him up, dear lady. Tell the ring woman there's a monster on her chimney, and she'll shoot him right off there!" Verny's translucent-green wings fluttered as he raised up into the air; doing circles and erratic dips before his mistress.

"She doesn't seem like the hunter type, so she'd probably become angry if I suggest shooting him down." Marit considered the situation for a moment. "I must find a way to make that woman trust me." She beckoned to Verny, and he landed atop her shoulder. "Let's go back home and get to the library. I need to learn more about the psychology of this planet's inhabitants."

"What about Baldrick?"

"If he keeps flying around in the open like that, someone will most certainly shoot him down. Forget about Baldrick."

The trio vanished.

Chapter 4

Jennifer spread out the landscape architect's drawings atop the card table. "Look at this … I'm getting a little waterfall and all kinds of good stuff!"

Brett leaned in to examine the plans. "It's wonderful! How did you find this talented man?"

"I called my realtor and she recommended him."

"This is going to be beautiful. You should give a party to show it off when it's done."

"I don't know anyone but you and Ophelia. I guess the three of us together could constitute a party."

"You grew up in California. Where are all your friends?"

"Well, you know … people change. When I left my husband, my friends were all married ladies who didn't want to associate with a single woman, so I learned how to be alone."

"I guess they weren't very good friends."

"I have no idea what was going on in their heads, so I don't know if the end of the friendships was their fault. It was probably mine. Like I said before, I'm not good with people."

The man tapped the plastic top of the card table with his fingertips. "If you decide you want to get some real furniture, I can help you shop. There's a couple of stores in town that sell furniture handmade by local craftspeople: solid, quality pieces that'll …"

"Ah! What's that?" A scrabbling noise was coming from one of the living room's fireplaces.

"Sounds like an animal is having an encounter with your chimney."

"I'd just as soon leave it be, but if it's stuck in there, I'll need to rescue it." Jennifer went to the fireplace. Bending down, she put her head inside the space over the hearth. "It sounds like something with serious claws is trapped in there." She stood upright. "I better go up and check it out."

"I'll go with you."

They ascended the main staircase, then went up a set of utility stairs providing access to the housetop. Stepping out onto a narrow walkway traversing the various peaks of the roof, the two looked at the chimney in question.

"Wow!" Brett said. "That's the biggest bird I've ever seen!"

"Oh, dear." Jennifer groaned.

A gigantic dark-blue bird was struggling to free itself. Most of the avian was inside the chimney: two kicking legs and the tips of of its wings were all that was visible.

“I don’t feel good about this,” Brett said. “Those bird legs are almost as long as mine.”

“If we just stand by in the hope that it’ll get itself out, it might get in there deeper and die.”

“I’d feel better about this if I knew what species it is. Maybe a great blue heron?”

“Maybe.” Jennifer grabbed a railing that served as a handhold for climbing the slope of the roof. “You stay there. If something bad happens, it would be best if it doesn’t happen to both of us, right?”

“Right.”

She made her way up to the chimney and stood a safe distance from the legs; hoping they would stop kicking. They went still a few seconds later and she lunged forward, grabbed both of them, and pulled with all her weight.

The bird came free in an instant and she fell backwards; landing on her rear end. Her head knocked against the railing and her eyes closed; opening again as she heard a thump.

Brett lay on the walkway face-up; his eyes closed. She climbed to her feet and started to go down to him.

“He fainted! Get out the smelling salts!”

She sat down hard. Gathering her courage, she turned around.

The bird was about six feet tall; covered in dark-blue feathers. There was a human face where avian eyes and a beak should have been, and attached to its shoulders, just in front of the attachments of the wings, were two feathered arms with long-clawed hands.

"You must help him! Get out the smelling salts!"

"Okay …" Jennifer cleared her throat. "Okay."

"What are you waiting for?"

"'Okay' is one of those things people say when they're at a loss for words. I am not getting out smelling salts."

"Why not?"

"Well … I don't have any, for one thing."

"All ladies always have smelling salts."

"This is the twenty-first century, bird."

"What does that have to do with anything?"

"Women don't go around fainting anymore."

"But clearly men do, so there is a need for such a medication." The bird blinked. "I'll go through his pockets; surely he has a bottle on him somewhere."

"No!"

"Why not?"

"Leave him alone. If he comes to and sees you poking around in his clothes, he'll lose his mind."

"You see me and you haven't lost your mind."

"Oh, I lost my mind quite some time ago. Since it's now gone, I can't very well lose it, can I?" She nodded vigorously. "Can't lose something I don't have!"

"If you insist, I will leave him be."

"I insist."

"Very well."

Jennifer grabbed the rail and rose to her feet. "How did you get stuck in my chimney?"

"I saw something shiny in there. I can't resist shiny things." The bird tilted his head to one side. "Aren't you going to ask about my point of origin? I don't believe you have creatures like me in this world. Don't you want to know from whence I have come?"

"I didn't think you would tell me if I asked, and I hate it when questions aren't answered."

"I will tell you if you take me into your home. I'm quite upset after being trapped in that chimney, and I require comforting."

"You require comforting?"

"Yes, please."

"Do you promise you'll leave when I ask you to?"

"Yes."

"Do you promise not to poop on my floor?"

"What is 'poop'?"

"The act of excreting … excrement."

"I would never do that indoors."

"All right."

The bird man smiled. "My name is Baldrick. What is your name?"

"Jennifer. The unconscious man is Brett."

"Shall I carry him indoors for you?"

"Refer to the response given earlier regarding you searching through his pockets."

"Shall we wait for him to wake up?"

"Tell you what … go hide behind the chimney so he can't see you, and I'll try to wake him up. When I get him back inside, I'll return for you."

"I'll hide and wait for your return." Baldrick went behind the chimney.

Jennifer knelt beside Brett and shook one of his shoulders. "Hey! Are you in there?" There was no response, so she tapped his forehead with her fingertips. "Brett!"

He opened his eyes. "Big bird with human face."

"Yeah, well; don't worry about that." She grabbed one of his hands and stood upright; helping him to his feet. "Let's get you inside."

There was no conversation as they descended to the ground floor of the house. They entered the office, and Brett took a chair. "Did I really see a big bird with a human face?"

"Yes. I'm going back up to the roof to fetch him. He wants to come inside."

"You're going to let him in your house?"

"He promised to tell me where he comes from. That's a story I want to hear!"

"Well … I guess if he turns dangerous, the two of us together can overpower him."

"Yes, we can." She patted his arm. "Just sit tight: I'll be right back."

"You don't have to coddle me. I suffered from a brief brain-glitch due to extreme stress and it won't happen again. I'm not a coward."

"I believe you."

BALDRICK stood in a sunny spot before the office window, looking at the stacks of books piled up next to the room's empty shelves. "Are these fiction, or are you a scholar studying something wonderful?"

"Fiction and history. I don't study history, exactly; I just like to read about it."

"Very nice, ma'am. They look new. All the books to which I have access are quite old."

"That explains your interest in smelling salts and aversion to ending a sentence with a preposition, I suppose."

Baldrick smiled and nodded.

"Spill the beans, dude."

The bird-man's brown eyes widened. "To which beans are you referring, ma'am?"

"She wants you to tell us your story."

"Yes, sir." He bent his legs and lowered himself into a sitting position. "I hail from Euromoss …"

"All hail Euromoss!" Jennifer's right hand shot into the air in a salute.

"Excuse me, ma'am?"

"I'm sorry. I'm trying not to take this seriously. It's my way of coping with stuff."

"Jennifer, there's a talking bird with a human face and arms sitting right in front of us. I think we should take this seriously."

"Sorry, Brett." She smiled. "Please continue, Baldrick. I promise to be polite."

"My home is not very different from this place. We have the same atmosphere, weather patterns, and terrain. Our evolutionary processes, however, move at a faster pace than yours. Those processes sometimes operate on a more personal level than yours as well."

"Personal level?"

"Evolution can be influenced by what individual sentient beings desire, instead of what is best for the species as a whole."

"That sounds like a bad thing," Brett said.

"It has led to some problems, but the sum total of them is no worse than the struggles facing your home."

"Is Euromoss a planet occupying the same universe as this one, or are you from a different dimension?"

"It's a different dimension, ma'am."

"How did you get here? A woman named Marit has been popping in and out of my house using what appears to be an ability to materialize and dematerialize at will. I assume she's from the same place as you. Do you just think, 'I'll go traveling,' and it happens?"

"Marit." Baldrick's eyes narrowed.

"You don't appear to be fond of her," Brett said.

"She is not a friend of mine." He fluffed out his feathers, then smiled and relaxed. "In answer to your question, ma'am, traveling is an internally triggered process for we who are known as 'Goers.' We can get about that way on both the physical plane and in between dimensions."

"Why have you come here?"

"I like to visit now and then, sir, just for pleasure. This is the only place I've found where I can both breathe in the atmosphere and speak the local language, which happily is the same as mine."

"You came to my house by random chance; not by choice?"

"Yes, ma'am."

"You're lying."

Baldrick's smile vanished. "Why do you make such a terrible accusation?"

"Marit showed up quite deliberately and was followed by you. That's not random."

"No, that was an accident! I was going after a shiny thing!"

"If that were the case, you could have easily freed yourself by dematerializing out of the chimney. You were putting on an act for my benefit." Jennifer uncrossed her folded legs and leaned forward in her chair. "You wanted me to feel sorry for you."

Baldrick's eyes darted back and forth. "I …"

"The ring isn't here. You're wasting your time."

The bird sighed. "I wasn't planning to steal it from you, ma'am. I hoped you might let me borrow it."

"I don't think I'll be doing that."

"I understand."

"Marit wants the ring, too, doesn't she?"

"Yes."

"That woman has a superior air about her that irritates me."

"She's quite proud of having the ability to appear as a giant. Her companions can also project an illusion of being something other than what they are in reality."

"The raven and the wolf?"

"That's how they appeared to you? Interesting."

"What are they really?"

"Verny's a dragon, and Fenright is a mixed-breed halfling. Both species are looked down upon in my world, so they developed the ability to temporarily appear as something else."

"That's sad." Brett frowned. "Pretending to be something else to avoid discrimination: that's awful."

"It's the way it is. Everyone needs to look down upon someone. The purebred humans consider all mixed breeds inferior, so we've created our own fairly stupid caste system wherein we pretend to be superior to the smaller, less powerful creature. Poor Verny: dragons are at the bottom of the heap."

"You have dragons in your world." Jennifer smiled. "That's so cool!"

"They're little winged snakes with stubby legs; not like the great fire-breathing beasts from your mythology." Two furry blurs flew past the door, and Baldrick trembled.

"It's just my cats."

"Are they dangerous?"

"Not usually."

"That's good."

"How did you come to know I have the ring?"

"I received this information on a second-hand basis, so it might not be perfectly accurate, but I heard that Marit came across evidence of its existence while she was observing a man in this area. She made his acquaintance but was unable to get the ring from him. I started following her a few days ago, and since she was spending so much time around your home, I assumed you are the ring's new owner."

"I wonder how she tracked me down and got the details about what I wished for and the bad result of that wish?"

"There was a bad result?" Brett said. "You didn't tell me about that."

"I'll explain it to you later."

"Marit's good at research and observation. I'm not sure how she gets so much information here, since she chooses to remain hidden, for the most part, and probably doesn't go about asking questions of strangers."

"If she knows our alphabet and all that, she could just read. Does she know how to use a computer?"

"Certainly."

"That explains it, then. Ain't nothing private anymore!"

"I don't mean to criticize, but you didn't exactly opt for anonymity when you decided to have yourself put on the list of the ten richest people in the world." Brett chuckled.

"My fault!" She smiled. "Hey, bird-man; are you hungry? Can I get you something?"

"You're not mad at me for wanting the ring?"

"Of course not. Who wouldn't want a magic ring? I can't blame you for that. If you'd invaded my privacy and carried out an elaborate campaign of deception, like Marit did, then I'd be mad. You did try to fool me, but you didn't try very hard."

Baldrick nodded. "I am hungry, ma'am; thank your for the offer."

"Go to the kitchen and eat whatever you like." Jennifer rose from her chair, followed by the bird-man, and pointed in the direction of that room. "You know about kitchens and refrigerators and all that?"

"Yes, ma'am."

She stood in the hallway watching as the creature trotted away on his long, spindly legs. When he turned a corner, she returned to her chair.

"Do you think it's a good idea to let him wander around in your house alone?" Brett frowned. "Would you let a stranger you just met on the street do that?"

"That depends on the stranger. I might … it's not like I have valuable things sitting around that anyone would want to steal. If he really needs my card table, he's welcome to it!"

"Where's your purse?"

"Oops … it's in the kitchen." She stood. "I shall return!"

Jennifer found Baldrick standing before the open fridge with his head inside. She grabbed her handbag from a countertop, slung the strap over her shoulder, and went to his side.

"Do you see anything you like in there?"

He pulled out a small plastic container. "I like the color of whatever's inside this."

"Cheddar cheese." She took the container from him, set it on the butcher-block table, and proceeded to carve off slices for him. "Here."

He accepted the offered slice and popped it into his mouth. "Oh, that's really good!" His eyes closed as he chewed; nodding with pleasure.

"I'll get you some crackers." She found a package in the cupboard and pulled out a few wafers of stone-ground wheat. "You put the cheese on top and then eat it."

"Oh, that's just perfect!" He swallowed the mouthful of food. "May I have some more?"

"Sure, eat as much as you like." She stepped away from the butcher block. "I'm going back to sit with Brett. When you're done eating, please come back to the office."

"Yes, ma'am."

"I'm Jennifer; not ma'am."

"Yes, Jennifer."

She returned to the office and seated herself. "I like that strange critter."

"He's certainly interesting, though I don't trust him as much as you do."

"I don't see how he can be a danger to me. He's big, but top-heavy. If he gives me any trouble, I'll just tip him over."

"That's one way of looking at it." Brett raised an eyebrow.

"He weighs a lot less than a horse, so I don't see why I should be afraid of him."

"A horse?"

"I'll have to tell you about my last job one of these days."

"Speaking of things you need to tell me about: what was the bad result of your wish?"

Jennifer looked down at the floor. "I asked for my money to come to me from criminals and CEOs whose companies use slave labor. I specified that no one would die as a result of my wish, but the man who owned this house lost his fortune and killed himself the same day I made my wish." She looked at Brett. "I think the universe arranged for me to buy this house so I would be constantly reminded that I am not only a thief, but a murderer as well."

"You think that, but you don't know it for certain. It could all be just coincidence."

"There's no denying that I'm no better than a thief." She blinked, holding back tears. "I'm a killer, too!"

"I don't believe it." Brett rose from his chair. "I didn't know or like Gerald—the dead man—well enough to be interested in what happened to him, but now I want to know. I'm going to do some digging. If there's a logical explanation for what happened to his money—and I'm sure there is—I will find it."

"Maybe."

"Don't give in to despair. I'll be in touch as soon I have some solid facts."

"Bye."

Chapter 5

Jennifer spread a sheet over the inflated bed positioned in a corner of the otherwise empty living room. "Do you need a blanket?"

"No, thank you. My feathers keep me warm at night."

"Okay."

Baldrick hopped onto the bed to try it out, and a hissing sound erupted from the air mattress. "Oh, my claws! Sorry!"

"I have a repair kit for punctures—I'll fix it. We need to trim the ends of your claws so they'll be blunted, then it won't happen again."

"That would be fine." He hopped off the bed.

The infernal bell rang. "Ack!" Jennifer went to the door and answered it. "Come on in, Brett."

He entered and pulled his phone from a pocket. "Please give me your number before I forget to ask for it again."

She provided the requested information.

"Email?"

She provided the address.

Baldrick came into view. "Hello, Brett."

"Hello." He put his phone away. "I thought you'd be gone by now."

"I've been given a position in this house." The bird-man smiled.

"What position?"

"Bodyguard and advisor to Jennifer."

"Oh."

A timer in the kitchen beeped. "My cheese dish is ready. Please excuse me."

"Okay." He watched Baldrick totter away. "You're letting him stay here?"

"Yeah. As much as I enjoy talking to Boris, it'll be nice to have conversations that aren't one-sided. Besides that, he can help me understand and deal with Marit. I don't think she's going to leave me alone just because I tell her to."

"Can't you just wish for her to leave you alone?"

"I expect to keep that ring for the rest of my life. I probably have a good fifty years ahead of me. With a limit of five wishes, I've decided to use it only once every ten years, unless a truly serious emergency forces me to deviate from that plan."

"You don't think Marit's presence poses the threat of a serious emergency?"

"Not yet. Baldrick's certain we can keep her at bay."

"What does he get in return for helping you?"

"He really does like shiny things, so I'm going to pay him with occasional gifts of antique silver. I ordered a

Queen Anne teapot for him. He's real excited about it."

"Are you sure it's safe to have him here?"

"Yeah. I'm not psychic, but my intuition is pretty good. If he was a bad guy, I'd feel it in my bones."

"All right." Brett smiled. "I have good news for you."

"Yes?"

"Gerald's assets were seized by the justice department in a civil forfeiture action. His money went to the government; not you."

She let out a sigh of relief. "Thank you." Her eyes closed. "That burden was too heavy." She looked at Brett. "Did he deserve to lose all his money?"

"He'd been committing fraud. He hurt a lot of people."

"Okay." Jennifer bit her lower lip. "That Marit creature let me think his death was my fault. Maybe she didn't know it wasn't the result of my wish, but I have a feeling she did. She must be really evil. If she were to ever get her hands on the ring, no good would come of it; that's for sure!" She paused. "How self-centered am I being, anyway? I didn't even ask how you are today."

"I'm fine, thank you. My mother is feeling better and I'm happy about that."

"What's been … why was she feeling bad?"

"My father passed away last year."

"I'm sorry."

"He'd been ill for a long time. I'm glad he's not suffering anymore, but my mother hasn't been able to adjust. I moved back in with her after his passing so she wouldn't be alone, but no one can replace my father."

"I can imagine how tough this would be for her."

"I've been encouraging her to help me manage their estate, and today, she finally showed some interest. My mother has a wonderful head for finance. The work will be good for her."

"I'm glad to hear that." Jennifer gestured toward the kitchen. "Would you like to have some cheese soufflé? We can sit and eat while you tell me more about your family."

"Thank you."

MARIT slammed the book shut; tilting her head back to avoid the dust drifting up from the aged volume. "This is no help at all!"

Fenright, seated in the chair next to hers, stroked her arm to soothe her. "Perhaps a different reference will be of more assistance?"

"All the books here are too old to be relevant, but the resources available through our computers are of such poor quality, I thought these might suffice. We should have stayed in the other world and gone into one of their libraries after they closed. I didn't have the patience to wait, so here I am; wasting my time."

"We can go back," Verny said.

"No." Marit shook her head, and Verny leaned to one side to avoid being swept off her shoulder. "I believe I've been going about this in the wrong manner. Ryan didn't trust me any more than Miss

Grace does, so I must accept the fact that the people of that world tend to disrespect me. A more direct means of obtaining the ring must be devised." She gazed at the stained-glass windows illuminating the reading room as she considered the matter; indifferent to the beauty of the bright-colored images of heroic figures from history. A life-sized portrait of the first man to succeed as a Goer between locations was positioned beside a panel depicting a female giant gazing down at a tiny warthog.

Choking sounds interrupted her thoughts, and she turned in her chair. A human figure topped with the head of an owl and dressed in a purple-velvet gown sat at a nearby table. She opened her mouth, which had lips rather than a beak, and out popped the exoskeleton of a cockroach.

"Can't you do that outside?" Marit glared at the woman.

"I expel indigestible materials when and where I must," she replied. "It's not something that can be planned, you know!"

"Disgusting." Marit turned away. "I'm surrounded by half-breeds. Where have all the purebreds gone?"

"I believe they're …"

"I know where they are, Fenright." She tapped her fingernails against the polished-mahogany tabletop. "Since psychological manipulation isn't going to work, I must use force. The question is, how can I use explosives to blow up a safe-deposit box without destroying the ring inside it?"

"Steal the key from the woman: it's as simple as that," Verny said.

"And how do I steal something when I don't know where it is?"

"If you could put the woman into a situation that forces her to make a wish, she would get the key from its hiding place and then you could steal it from her."

"That sounds like an extremely complicated scheme. Also … she might be stronger than I am. I'm not sure I could overpower her."

"Get a gun," Fenright said. "Everybody in the other world has a gun, so it should be easy to steal one. All you have to do is go into her house, point the gun at her, and demand that she give you the key."

"I like that idea." She patted the halfling's head. "Good boy."

"I think you should wait until nightfall. I believe people usually steal things in the dark."

"They probably do just that." Marit nodded. "We should go for a walk while we wait for night to arrive. If I don't move about in the old way every now and then, my leg muscles will become weak. First, I'll need shoes." She put a hand on Fenright's head.

The trio rematerialized inside Marit's home. Verny flew to a glass dish sitting in a corner and took a long drink of water. Fenright … well, he didn't exactly walk across the floor of the one-room house. He did use his legs like a biped, occasionally dropping the knuckles of one fist onto the carpet to steady himself, but his movements were more like the scrambling of a spider than a strolling human.

He went to the small refrigerator and opened the door. "May I have some cold oat mush, dear lady?"

"Yes, you may." Marit smiled. "Since you came up with the wonderful idea about using a gun, you may also have as many dried grapes and as much sugar as you like."

"Thank you!" He pulled a covered bowl from the fridge and proceeded to prepare his meal.

Marit's home was a pleasant enough place. The one room encompassing the kitchen, sitting area, sleeping space and bathing facilities was clean and quite large. The furnishings were plain and unexceptional, save the full-length standing mirror whose frame was ornately carved and covered with a gleaming layer of gold leaf.

She went to it and examined her reflection. Using a silver-backed brush, she smoothed her hair. Removing her bracelets, she set them on a table and rubbed away the green stains they had left on her arms.

A wooden rack holding hanging clothes stood in one corner. She went to it and pulled off a long, loose dress of black satin. After changing into it, she dug around in a chest of drawers and extracted a pair of flat brown shoes.

"Are you going to deliver important documents while you are out and about, dear lady?" Verny asked.

"It's too late in the day for business." Marit threw a green shawl over her shoulders. "The Founders' Week celebrations start tomorrow, so I shall be free to do as I wish for the next eight days. We will make the most of this holiday, boys."

She went to the door of the dwelling and opened it. "You will behave yourselves while I'm gone, won't you?"

"Yes, dear lady!" they replied.

She descended the front stairs of the brick building and stepped onto the road. The late-afternoon sunlight shining on her face made it hard for her to see, so she lowered her gaze onto the cobblestones of the narrow city street; keeping her eyes on the oft-perilous footing of the unmaintained pavement.

A loud clomping came up behind her, and she moved aside to let the horse and rider pass. A hand on her shoulder made her gasp and turn around.

"Konrath, don't sneak up on me like that!"

"I wasn't sneaking."

"You should speak to a woman rather than touching her when she doesn't know you're there."

The tall man smiled and removed his bowler hat; smoothing his white hair with a gray-gloved hand. "Are you out for some exercise?"

"Yes."

"May I join you?"

"What are you doing on my street?"

"I was about to knock on your door when I saw you here on the road."

"What do you want?"

"How are you today?"

"You came here to find out how I am? That seems unlikely."

The pair leaned up against the wall of an apartment building to avoid being crushed by a passing horse-drawn van. "You've been going on excursions to that other place."

"That's no concern of yours."

"I hope you're being careful."

"There's nothing for me to fear … I can move about there as easily I do here."

"If a stressful situation causes your powers of concentration to weaken, you could be trapped in a foreign world. What would become of you then?"

"I don't appreciate your habit of creeping about inside my mind to gather information about my personal movements. If you continue with that practice against my will, I shall inform the Council of Mind-Readers."

"I will respond to that action by telling the Lord High Chief of the Goers that you're traveling outside our territory in order to obtain a ring that can provide you with a dangerous amount of power."

"So, you're the one who started that rumor!" Marit stepped into the middle of the road. "You have no proof of such a ring and will not be believed."

"I am known for the veracity of my character and precise perceptive abilities, while you are notoriously self-centered and devious. I will be believed; you shall not." Konrath smiled. "If I report you to the Lord Chief, he will enlist the aid of our interrogatory force and they will look into your mind to see your lies. You know that!"

"Goodbye." She strode to the end of the street and turned onto the main avenue of the city.

The lanes for non-pedestrian traffic were crowded with riders, horse-drawn vehicles, cars, and motorcycles. Marit cringed as she joined in with the humans and half-breeds traveling on foot. A reptile-faced man in a royal-blue brocade suit drew near; his arm brushing against hers as he passed by.

Marit shuddered. After enduring several similar incidents of close contact with mixed-breed creatures, the woman took a deep breath and willed herself back home.

"You're back already, dear lady?" Fenright scrambled to her side.

She looked down at him. "When the ring and the other world are mine, I shall give you a body worthy of your sweet nature."

"I am honored that you would use one of your precious wishes to benefit me, dear lady." He rubbed his head against her leg.

"After I have my evening meal, we'll get back to the other world. Before this night ends, I will have the ring!" She stroked Fenright's head. "Please see to the cooking."

"Yes, dear lady."

BRETT AND Jennifer took seats on the repaired and re-inflated air bed as Baldrick settled down on the floor.

"You have people other than yourself in your home now, Jennifer … may I include you in the 'people' category, Baldrick?"

"Certainly, sir."

"As I was saying … you're no longer a solitary hermit. Isn't it about time you got some furniture?"

"I guess so, but it seems like such a commitment. Being burdened with possessions would, uh, kind of remind me of being married."

"Not a good experience for you, I take it?"

"Nope. I suppose I shouldn't blame everything on my ex, but I do. He had a cocaine habit and no interest in giving it up."

"Oh."

Jennifer cleared her throat. "Anyway, my ex's habit was driving me crazy and I had a stupid response to it. I told him I wanted a divorce right after I was laid off from a new job."

"That seems like a bad time to split up," Brett said.

"I'd run out of rope; as in I had absolutely none left to grab onto. We were having a nasty argument and I lost control of my mouth."

"I see."

"He ordered me to get out of the house. Since he was bigger and stronger than me, I packed a bag, got into my car, and left. I had almost no money and nowhere to go. I lived in my car for a while, but that was horrible, so I tried a homeless shelter. They let me sleep on the top level of a bunk bed in a huge room packed full of strangers. When I got up in the morning, I saw signs posted on the walls telling people not to attack other people or engage in public sex. I mean … think about that! Would you want to sleep in a place where signs like that are necessary?"

Brett's eyes opened wide, and he shook his head.

"That would make me very uncomfortable," Baldrick said.

"Needless to say, I did not spend another night there."

There was a period of awkward silence before Jennifer spoke again. "I guess it's kind of shocking for you to learn that your new neighbor used to be homeless."

"I am surprised, but you know … all it takes is one mistake or stroke of bad luck and a person's life can fall completely apart. Before my father passed away, my mother was active in charities for the homeless, and she told me about people whose stories are similar to yours."

"Yeah."

"How did you get out of, uh, living in your car?"

"I looked for jobs at the library and found one that offered a place to live. I had childhood experience with horses, so I qualified for the position Linda was offering. I was lucky to get it." She nodded. "I was really lucky."

Baldrick straightened his legs and stood. "I believe you should have some ice cream, Jennifer. We should all have some ice cream. I'll go get it." He headed for the kitchen.

"I'm guessing you don't want to furnish this house because you're expecting to lose it at any moment," Brett said. "This is your home, and no one's going to kick you out or take it away from you."

"While my brain knows that's probably true, my heart fears and expects the worst."

"Time will take care of that problem, I imagine. For now, all I can say is that it would make me very happy if you'd allow me to take you shopping for furniture tomorrow."

"I'll think about it."

"That's a start."

Marit and her companions regarded the barred windows of the gun store. "That place is scary," the tiny dragon said. "I don't want to go in there—it looks like a prison."

"Fenright, you'll stay here and protect Verny. This won't take much time, I hope."

She willed herself into the shop and waited a few seconds as her vision adjusted to the darkness. "Oh, fascinating!" An array of deadly weapons surrounded her: dozens of rifles and shotguns barrel-up in racks against the walls; glass display cases packed with handguns.

"Bigger is better." She looked over the long-barreled firearms and selected a semiautomatic rifle. "Oh, it's heavy!"

Pressing it to her chest, she tried to make her exit from the building and failed. The unfamiliar object wasn't as easy to transport as her two companions; requiring an intense level of concentration.

'I can do this!' she thought. 'The first time's always the hardest with a new foreign object.'

Taking a deep breath, she put all her energy into the effort and found herself outside.

"Ow!" Fenright let out a yelp: Marit had materialized onto his foot.

"My apologies." She stepped back and freed his appendage. "The weapon threw off my bearings."

"It's a nice one, isn't it? Nice and big!"

Marit nodded. "I wonder if we should go back to the library so I can research how to use it. I don't know; it seems pretty simple. Just raise it up, point the end at the person who needs persuading, and press that little curved piece of metal if she refuses to cooperate."

"That will make her dead, you know," Verny said.

"I know."

Chapter 6

Jennifer watched as Baldrick loaded the dishwasher. "You didn't agree to do all this cooking and cleaning when we set the terms of your employment. I think I should pay you more than our original agreement."

"One piece of beautiful silver every week is enough to make me happy, thank you. I enjoy cooking and cleaning, anyway. I performed all the domestic chores for my family before my mother remarried. Her new husband does it now."

"Shouldn't you let your family know where you are?"

"They won't start to worry for a while yet. I told them I'd be coming here for an adventure, so they don't expect to hear from me for some time."

"All right. Well, I'm tired and going to bed. If you're planning to watch movies on my computer, please use the headset so the noise won't wake me."

"I'll do that." Baldrick turned on the dishwasher and headed for the office.

Jennifer ascended the stairs and entered her bedroom. Switching on the light, she was pleased to see both cats sleeping on the blue and white patchwork quilt, with Boris curled up against the older feline's belly. "Nice adjustment to the new territory, Natasha," she whispered.

She sat on the end of the mattress, moving carefully to avoid waking the cats. Bending forward, she pulled off her sandals and set them on the floor.

As she raised her head, she saw the toes of two bare feet peeking out from under the white cloth of Marit's usual attire. Sitting up straight, she stared into the barrel of the rifle the woman held.

"Please don't hurt my cats," she whispered.

"I won't hurt anyone if you give me the key to your safe-deposit box."

"Okay." Jennifer, trembling with apprehension, walked to a bureau and opened the top drawer. She pulled out a small white envelope with the words *Lockbox Key* written on the front.

"Toss it over here."

Jennifer threw the envelope across the room. When it landed at Marit's feet, the lady smiled and pointed the rifle barrel at the sleeping cats. There was a sound of metal clicking against metal, repeated over and over. The clicking stopped, and the blonde shook the weapon with both hands. "What's wrong with this thing?"

"You forgot to load it!" Jennifer ran forward and threw herself onto the villain, knocking her off her feet. "You tried to kill my cats!" Sitting atop Marit's stomach, she punched the blonde's face twice. When a bit of blood leaked from the corner of the woman's mouth, she came to her senses. "Okay; that's enough." She rose to her feet and stood a few yards away. Panting heavily, she glared at the woman lying on the floor.

Marit, her eyes half-closed, groped about on the carpet until she felt the envelope. Seizing it, she took a deep breath.

Jennifer watched as the woman became slightly transparent, shimmered back to solid, then disappeared. "That's interesting; I think she had trouble gettin' outta here. I'll have to consult Baldrick about that." She was speaking to the cats; unaware that they were both under the bed.

She noticed the gun lying on the floor. "Oh, crap! I can't keep that—I don't own it, and I don't have a license. Just having it here is against the law. Oh, crap!"

Jennifer went downstairs and found Baldrick sitting at the desk in her office; staring at the computer screen in fascination. The headset he wore indicated that he was watching a film. She approached him and tapped on his shoulder.

He removed the headset and turned away from the action flick. "Yes?"

"Marit was just here. She tried to shoot Boris and Natasha!"

"What?"

"The gun wasn't loaded, so everybody's okay."

"She just came in to kill your pets?"

"Not exactly. She came to get the key to the lockbox where I keep the ring."

"Did she get it?"

"I gave it to her, but the bigger problem is that she left her gun behind. I need to call the security folk and tell them somebody left a semiautomatic rifle in my house."

"Why is that a bigger problem?"

"Security will probably search the house and yard looking for the intruder who left it here, and it wouldn't be a good thing for you to be here. You should go outside and perch in the top of a really tall tree so they won't see you. I'm going to make the call right now."

"But she's going to get the ring!"

Jennifer chuckled. "Don't worry about that; just get yourself outta here."

MARIT MATERIALIZED onto the lawn behind the house. Her waiting companions, seeing her lying there, rushed to her side.

"Are you all right?" Verny beat his wings and hovered over her, swooping and dipping like an oversized hummingbird.

"You're bleeding, dear lady!" Fenright stroked her cheek.

"That doesn't matter. I got the key!" She sat up, holding the envelope in one hand, and tore it open. "There's the key and a piece of paper." She read the receipt. "Here's the address of the bank and the box number." She jumped to her feet, grinning. "To the library for maps we shall go, and then the ring is mine!"

Verny landed atop her shoulder. She put a hand on the halfling's head, and the trio disappeared.

A short time later, they stood before the bank. "Will we be safe out here while you're inside?" The dragon left the woman's shoulder and perched atop Fenright's head. "I don't like this street. The structures are all too big and nasty-looking." He shivered. "Too many shiny buildings."

"They won't hurt you as long as you don't go flying into one of those big windows," Fenright said.

"I don't know how long it will take me to find the box. You boys should hide somewhere safe." Marit went to the entrance of the bank and tried the locked door. "Hmm … that device there indicates that I can get inside if I put a bank card in the slot. I wonder if I can get out without using one?" In a second, she was inside the chamber containing the automatic-teller machines. She pushed the door handle and smiled as the portal opened. "Come inside, boys. You'll be safe in here, and if anything unexpected happens, you can get out on your own."

"Don't speak of unexpected things!" Verny shook his head and whimpered.

"I'll return soon."

Marit vanished and reappeared in the middle of the customer-service seating area. Scanning her surroundings, she looked for a sign indicating the location of the lockboxes. Seeing none, she decided to gain entrance to the most clearly fortified part of the bank.

Materializing into the vault, she was delighted to find herself surrounded by small brass doors bearing numbers. "It's here!" She located Jennifer's box, reached into a pocket of her gown, and removed the envelope containing the key.

Trembling with excitement, she pulled out the key, then froze. "Why are there two key holes? Must I unlock it twice?" She took a deep breath and inserted the key into a lock. It fit. She tried the other hole. It did not fit.

Dropping the useless key, she fell to her knees and shouted curses at the floor. As she raised her head to scream at the ceiling, a blinking red light high up in a corner caught her attention. "I must get my boys out of here!"

She willed herself into the bank foyer. "We have to leave. Law enforcement will surely be on their way."

Verny flew onto her shoulder, and she put a hand on Fenright's head. As she concentrated, the trio became semitransparent for a second, then hard solidity reasserted itself.

Marit heard sirens wailing in the distance. "Run!" She opened the door, and they fled into the night.

Jennifer stopped in the driveway; seeing Brett approaching the front door of her home. He turned and walked to her car as she lowered the window.

"Don't you ever turn on your phone?" he asked.

"I do when there's an emergency."

Movements in the backseat caught his attention. "Who's that?"

"His name is Baskerville. You can call him Basker if you want."

"He's huge!"

"Yeah! When he stands up on his hind legs, he's seven feet tall." Jennifer laughed. "He's not only big; he moves really fast."

"What breed?"

"Irish wolfhound."

"Won't he eat your cats?"

"No, he lived with cats at his former home."

"Where did you get him?"

"I went to a rescue place for large dogs that's real careful about who they allow to adopt. They checked out my identity and made me prove I have a big yard and proper fencing for this guy, enough money to feed and care for him, and an air-conditioned house: wolfhounds don't do well in hot summers." She grinned. "He's smart, and his powers of observation are super-sharp. He can differentiate between friend and foe in an instant and make his own decision about how to respond to a threat. He's a sighthound, which means he has superior vision and short-term speed for sprinting. And I think I'd better shut up before I bore you to death singing his praises." She turned off the engine and got out of the car. “I’ll introduce you to him.”

When she opened a rear door of her sedan, a gigantic yet elegant dog covered in shaggy gray fur stepped out. He was interested in his new surroundings but calm; possessing the innate confidence peculiar to huge creatures.

“He has a wise face.”

“Put out your hand, Brett.” Jennifer smiled at the dog. “Basker, this is Brett. Shake!”

The dog raised his paw, and the grinning man shook it. “I like him!”

“I do, too.”

“Is this adoption a response to whatever happened at your house last night? I saw the patrol vehicles here.”

“Yeah, I thought I could use some more security. I was up all night looking at dog websites.”

“Are you going to tell me what happened?”

“Marit popped into my bedroom with an assault rifle and took one of the keys to my safe-deposit box.”

“An assault rifle? Wow! Was anyone hurt?”

“No.”

“That was fortunate, to say the least.” Brett shook his head. “I guess she didn’t know about the need for a bank employee with a second key.”

“Nope. She also didn’t seem to know that guns need bullets.”

“Lucky for you!”

“She tried to shoot my cats. I punched her a couple of times.”

"Good."

Jennifer reached into the car, pulled out a leash, and clipped it onto Basker's collar. "Come inside and I'll tell you about the chink in Marit's armor."

The bank manager stared at her computer. She replayed the video over and over; watching Marit appear and disappear as two bizarre creatures moved about inside the ATM lobby.

She sighed. "The world just keeps on getting weirder."

"HERE'S YOUR mail." Baldrick set a stack of envelopes on the desk before Jennifer.

"Thank you."

"Where's Brett?"

"He went home."

"I like your dog. Can I take him out for a walk?"

"No, unless you possess the magical power to make yourself look like an ordinary human being."

"It's not magic, but I can't do that."

"When it gets dark, you can take him into the backyard and play with him. That is, if you want to."

"I do. Come along and help me cook, Basker!" The dog rose to his feet and the two creatures trotted out of the room.

Jennifer sorted through the envelopes; putting bills in one stack and advertisements in a second. There were two personal letters bearing return addresses she didn't recognize. She picked up the first letter and opened it. Reading the page, she saw it was a letter addressed to the previous occupant of the house. "I shouldn't be reading this guy's private mail. I'll have it returned to sender." She put it aside.

As she read the second letter from the stack, her eyes opened wide. "Well, I'll be darned!" She jumped up from her chair and ran to the kitchen.

Baldrick looked up from the pile of carrots he was chopping. "Is there something interesting in that letter you're waving?"

"Yes! It's from Ryan; the guy who owned the ring before me!"

"Ah … he should have some good stories to tell us. Invite him to dinner and I'll give him some of my good soup."

"I'll feel him out to see if he can handle meeting you. If he can, I'll give him the invite."

She ran back to her office, picked up the phone sitting on her desk, and dialed the number provided in the letter.

A few minutes later, Jennifer returned to the kitchen. "He can handle you, Baldrick, and he'll be here for dinner tonight."

"Wonderful! I'll bake some nice rolls to go with the soup."

"That's a good idea."

Returning to her office, she was just beginning to read the online news when the phone rang. "Hello?"

"Ms. Grace?"

"Yes."

"I'm Alice Parker; the manager of your bank."

"Hi."

"I want to let you know we found a key for your safe-deposit box in the vault."

"Oh."

"Would you like to come by and pick it up?"

"Sure. I'll come over right now."

"Thank you."

After Jennifer's identity had been thoroughly verified by a bank employee, she was ushered into the manager's office. A red-haired woman in a black suit sat at a desk; rising to her feet as the visitor approached. She smiled. "Ms. Grace."

"Ms. Parker."

The two women shook hands.

"Please have a seat."

Jennifer took one of the chairs near the desk as the manager returned to hers.

Ms. Parker opened a drawer and took out a small envelope, then looked into Jennifer's eyes. "How did your key come to be in our vault?"

"I don't know."

"Was it stolen from you?"

"Yes."

"Do you know anything about the person who took it?"

"I reported the theft to the police last night."

"I'm glad you did that, but you didn't answer my question."

"No, I didn't." Jennifer smiled.

"It's unusual for someone to gain entrance to our vault in the middle of the night."

"I'm glad to hear that. I'd hate to think people go in and out of there whenever they like."

Ms. Parker closed her eyes for a moment and sighed. "I would greatly appreciate any information you can give me about the woman in the vault."

Jennifer sensed a painful level of desperation in the lady. "You know it was a woman."

"Yes."

"You saw her on the surveillance cameras?"

"Yes."

"I'm sorry to hear that."

"You know who she is, don't you?"

"Yes."

"Please explain!"

"I would rather not."

"I'm not the only person who saw the videos. What are we supposed to think?"

"Don't think about it. Just write it off as one of those 'there are more things in heaven and earth, Horatio' situations. Forget about it."

"I saw a small dragon flying around in my ATM lobby. I'm supposed to forget about that?"

"Ah, you saw Verny." Jennifer nodded. "Well, that's better than watching a fire-breathing dragon the size of Godzilla trash your bank, don't you think?"

Ms. Parker responded with an intense glare.

"Can I have my key, please? I have some transactions to carry out here, and then I must attend to an impending dinner party." Jennifer stood and held out one hand.

The redhead gave her the envelope.

"Thanks. Have a nice day!"

A roaring carburetor-powered monster could be heard rolling up the driveway. Jennifer opened the front door, and a pale-yellow Depression-era Duesenberg pulled up and parked before the house.

A young man emerged from the car. "Hi, Jenny!"

"If you want me to ignore you, just keep calling me that."

"Sorry." Ryan grinned.

"It's all right; a lot of people make that mistake."

"Okay."

Jennifer looked over the grand vehicle. "Doesn't driving such a rare, obviously valuable car make you feel, well … vulnerable?"

"I'm invulnerable."

"Oh, dear."

He chuckled. “I only drive it on special occasions. The ignition doesn’t lock, so I have to be careful where I park it.”

“I see.” She nodded. “Another question: who thought it was a good idea to give the ring to a teenaged boy?”

“I’m not a teenager.”

“You look to be around eighteen at most.”

“I’m sixty-eight.”

“Oh, dear.”

He grabbed his long black ponytail and shook it. “This used to be stone-gray.”

“Oh, dear.”

“You say that a lot.”

“I’d say the situation warrants it.”

“Ha!”

“I’m forgetting my manners.” Jennifer walked towards the open doorway. “Please, come inside.”

Ryan bounded up onto the porch and jogged through the house, stopping in the empty living room. “Nice! With all this space, you can throw some killer parties.”

“That’s not gonna happen.”

“Hold on a sec.” He pulled a phone from a pocket and looked at the screen. After a few taps at the device, he put it away and smiled at Jennifer. “You strike me as the sober type.”

“I suppose I am.”

“Where’s the kitten?”

“He’s probably on my bed with his new buddies. I got an older cat from the shelter to keep him company. After Marit showed up with a gun, I acquired an Irish wolfhound. He likes cats a lot, and they like him."

"Marit had a gun? Wow—she's getting desperate."

"Yeah."

"She didn't get the ring from you, did she?"

"No, I have it in a lockbox at the bank."

"That's what I did with it, too."

"Hello!"

Ryan turned around and spotted Baldrick. "Wow! You're incredible!"

"Thank you. You are incredible as well." The bird-man frowned. "Being incredible is a good thing, is it not?"

"It's good."

"Dinner is served. Are you ready to dine?"

"Yes!"

They followed Baldrick to the dining area. The card table was covered by a folded bed sheet, and three bowls of steaming soup sat atop it. A basket contained the fresh-baked rolls the bird-man had crafted by hand.

"This smells great!"

"Thank you. Please take a seat, sir."

"You can call me Ryan."

"I am Baldrick."

They sat at the table; each human putting a paper napkin on their lap. Baldrick couldn't fit into a chair and perched atop a short-legged stool. Having no lap, he left his napkin on the table.

Jennifer picked up her spoon. "Please eat!"

They ate in silence for a bit before Baldrick spoke. "Ryan, would you be comfortable telling us for what you wished?"

"Oh, sure; I don't mind at all." He set down his glass of water. "First thing, of course, was lots of money."

"Of course. One's basic needs must be met."

"Next, I was having health problems caused by age. I thought, if I wish to be healthy, I'll keep getting older and develop more problems that would use up all my wishes, so I asked for the body I had when I was seventeen. I specified that my body would never get old."

"Oh, dear!" Jennifer said. "How will you explain that to people who notice that you're not aging?"

"I'll tell them the truth; why not?"

"Oh, dear."

Ryan laughed. "There you go again!"

"Are you planning to live forever?"

"Yes. My third wish was immortality, hence my earlier statement about being invulnerable."

"You're going to get bored eventually, don't you think?"

"Oh, no! I love life, and it just keeps getting better."

"I'm sorry, but I don't think that was a good idea at all. What if the world becomes a horrible place to live?"

"That's not going to happen."

"You have no way of knowing what the future will bring."

"He made his decision, Jennifer. I don't believe finding fault with it can accomplish anything good." Baldrick took a bite of a roll.

"You're right." She bowed her head. "I'm sorry, Ryan."

"That's okay."

"If you want to tell us about your other wishes," Baldrick said, "I am certain no one will criticize your choices."

"Okay. My fourth wish will remain a secret, but I can tell you about the last one. My nephew's son had brain cancer." Ryan smiled. "He doesn't have it anymore!"

"Oh, that's terrific!" Jennifer said.

"Yeah!"

"Good choice." Baldrick took a sip of water. "That was noble and unselfish."

"Well, I couldn't stand by and watch a child die now, could I?"

"I guess not." Jennifer paused for a moment. "There weren't any bad … shall I say, side effects from any of your wishes?"

"Side effects?"

"You know—the monkey's paw thing. You get what you ask for but something awful happens in the process."

"If anything awful happened, I don't know about it."

"That's good. I thought I had killed someone, but it turned out I didn't."

"Wow. That would be hard to live with."

"It was awful for the brief period of time that I believed it. Marit encouraged me to think I'd killed someone."

"I was relieved she left me alone after I passed the ring on to you, though I'm sorry you're being burdened with her unexpected visits."

"Yeah."

"She tried really hard to get me to say where you lived, but that woman is so transparent … there was no way I was going to give you up to her."

"Thank you. It's fortunate that she didn't locate me until after I'd locked up the ring."

"Yes, it is," Baldrick said. "The rumors I heard suggest that she wants to use it to take over this world and make it her own."

"What?" Jennifer's jaw dropped. "You didn't tell me that!"

"I didn't think it was important. You're going to do your best to keep her from getting the ring no matter what she might do with it; is that not correct?"

She stared at her half-empty soup bowl. "That makes me even more determined to avoid taking it out of its lockbox. She might appear right beside me and snatch it, and that'll be the end of our world as we know it."

"She can only do that if she knows you're going to the box and follows you," Ryan said.

"I could wish for her to get permanently lost, but I won't do that. I'm not wasting wishes on a problem I can probably solve myself when I could be using them to do great things like what you did for that little boy."

"That's understandable."

"Do you know anything about her history? I'd like to think there's some kind of reason for her behavior; something that forced her to become, well, evil."

"She was unwilling to reveal anything about herself to me."

"What about you, Baldrick? Do you know anything about her background?"

"Marit has a long-standing reputation as a dishonest, selfish, and cruel woman. Rumors suggest she was born that way. I've met her mother and father, and they appear to be kind people with decent standards of ethics."

Clawed feet moving across the floor could be heard: Basker had come downstairs. He crossed the dining area and went to a window looking onto the backyard, where he stopped and stood still; staring into the distant trees and growling.

Jennifer regarded her canine protector. "The hound of the Baskervilles will keep us safe," she said. "Let's finish this delicious soup before it gets cold."

CHAPTER 7

Marit stood in the trees behind Jennifer's house. The pistol she held was loaded.

The dragon leaned to one side to whisper in her ear. "Are you certain your Goer abilities won't fail you again?"

"Yes, Verny; don't worry. I'll be fine. There's nothing that can upset me now. I have bullets, so she will give me both keys or I will kill her and her cats."

"Cats? You would kill cats?" Fenright moved away from the woman's side.

"They're creatures of no consequence. Why shouldn't I kill them?"

"Cats are small and soft, and their purring is delightful."

"I don't want them in that house while I'm living there."

"Can't you simply chase them away?"

"Shooting them is easier."

Fenright shook his head.

The Duesenberg's roaring engine could be heard. "Ryan is leaving," Marit said.

"Are you certain that's his automobile?" Verny asked.

"Yes, it's definitely Ryan's car."

"She'll be alone now, except for the two felines."

"I'll wait until her bedroom light goes on and then off. When she's in bed and falling asleep, I will strike."

JENNIFER put on her flannel nightgown and walked towards the bed. Her three pets were asleep on one side of the mattress, leaving just enough room for her to crawl in under the quilt. She moved carefully, trying to avoid waking the animals.

Laying her head down on the pillow, she reached out and put a hand against the wolfhound's head. Contact with a warm, furry body made falling asleep much easier.

As her eyes were closing, she saw a female form appear before the window. "Basker!" she shouted.

The wolfhound was awake and on top of the knocked-down lady in a split second. "Hold!" Jennifer rose from the bed and turned on a light. As she walked towards Marit, Baldrick trotted into the room.

"Would you please pick up that gun, Baldrick? I don't want my fingerprints on it when the police come to pick it up."

"I can do that." He retrieved the gun at Marit's side and put it on a table. "If you ask Basker to free her, she might recover from the shock and disappear, so don't do that."

"I don't want him to stand over her like that for very long; it's unkind."

"Unkind to the dog or the woman?"

"The dog. I couldn't care less about the woman."

"I can keep her here, if you like. She can't travel with another Goer holding her back."

"Really? That's good."

"Before I take over for Basker, I need to see to her companions. They're vulnerable without Marit at their side." He bent down to look at her face. "Where are Verny and Fenright?"

The words coming out of the terrified woman's mouth were incomprehensible.

"Are they in the backyard?"

"Yes!"

"I'll fetch them. Don't allow Basker to let go of her." Baldrick vanished; reappearing moments later with Verny and Fenright. "You fellows must stay in that corner." He pointed to an area a good distance from Marit, and they went to it. "Let me grab her ankle, then you can let the dog go his way."

Jennifer stood waiting until Baldrick, sitting on the floor beside Marit, had gripped one of her ankles with a strong hand. "Release!"

The wolfhound did as he was told. Going to the bed, he poked his nose under it. Both cats were hiding there; not at all interested in coming out. Abandoning his attempt to reach the felines, the dog stretched out on the floor and stared at Marit.

"I'm gonna get right to the point, woman," Jennifer said. "You can't get into that safe-deposit box. I suppose you thought I had the second key, but I don't: the bank has it. Don't for one second think you can go charging into that bank with a gun and demand the second key. I don't know what banks are like in your world, but here … that will get you killed." She bent down and poked Marit's forehead with a finger. "Get it? Leave me alone!"

"She'll leave you alone if you shoot her with that little gun," Fenright said.

Jennifer straightened up and looked at the halfling. "What?"

"Shoot her. She said she was going to kill your cats. I like cats. I don't like people who kill them." Fenright shook his head. "No, I don't like them at all!"

"I never thought you'd turn against your mistress, halfling." Baldrick turned to look at him.

Marit raised herself up and punched the bird-man's head. Stunned, he lost his grip on her ankle, and she vanished.

"Are you okay?"

"I'm sorry, Jennifer, and I'm fine." Baldrick rubbed the side of his head where he'd been struck. "At least you said what needed to be expressed while you had the chance. Other than following the halfling's recommendation, I don't see what else could have been done."

"You're right." She looked at the pair in the corner. "What shall become of these guys?"

"I could take them back to their home."

"No! I don't wish to return there. Without Marit's charity, I have nowhere to stay. I'll have to live on the streets, and I will probably starve." Fenright offered his arm to the dragon, who jumped up from the floor and perched on it. "What do you have to say, Verny?"

"The dear lady will be very angry about losing this little battle, and angrier still at your abandonment of her. It's not safe for me to be in her home at this time."

"She would hurt you because she's mad at someone else?"

"Yes, ma'am."

"Please don't call me that. My name is Jennifer."

"Yes, Jennifer."

"I guess we have some new roommates, Baldrick. What do you think?"

"They must earn their keep."

"That seems reasonable."

"I could take care of the cats for you," Fenright said.

"That would be helpful," Baldrick said, "but cleaning litter boxes and feeding the cats twice a day isn't much of a job, even if you include feeding the dog as well. Do you know anything about keeping a garden in order?"

"I don't think he should be spending time outside where people can see him. Not that you're unattractive, Fenright, but we don't have creatures like you here and I don't want the locals to, uh … well … they'd be freakin' out at the sight of you."

"You're forgetting about his ability to shield his identity with a false image."

"Oh, yeah!" She turned to the halfling. "Can you handle pulling weeds and cutting grass?"

"Most certainly, yes!"

"Okay. What about you, Verny? Do you have any skills or talents?"

"No." He lowered his head and stared at the floor.

"You can be a pet, I suppose."

"I am an excellent and extraordinary pet."

Jennifer smiled.

A tiny white head emerged from under the bed, and Boris crept forward to inspect the strangers. Fenright put out a hand and stroked him as Verny floated down to the floor and, creeping forward with great caution, approached the kitten. "Be nice, cat," the winged serpent said. Boris crouched down in a playful fashion, his tail swishing, and Verny jumped up, landing on the feline's back, then flapped his wings and took off. They began to play; the cat chasing the low-flying dragon about the big room.

Jennifer giggled. "A talking dragon's playing with my kitten! This is too cool!" She clapped her hands and laughed.

Marit stood before the mirror combing her hair. After braiding it into two thick ropes, she went to her dress rack and selected her finest gown: a form-fitting bias-cut sheath of shining gold lamé. She put it on and went to her bed; pulling a small wooden box from beneath it. Opening the container, she withdrew a heavy chain-mail bib of hand-worked silver set with sparkling yellow gems.

She returned to the mirror and connected the jewelry's silver cables at the back of her neck. Smoothing the dress over her hips, she smiled at her reflection. "I am truly irresistible," she whispered.

A small purse covered in silver beads sat atop a table near her, and she picked it up. After arranging the train at the back of the gown, she took a deep breath and vanished.

Marit reappeared before a pair of tall brass doors. The marble pavement of the mansion's porch was cold against the soles of her bare feet, and a cool breeze chilled her exposed arms.

She turned to admire the stately homes surrounding this home; appreciating the beauty and quiet of the fashionable neighborhood. Inhabited by only the highest members of the nobility, the area was off-limits to motorized traffic. A lone carriage moved along the pedestrian-free street; pulled by two huge, well-bred black horses walking at a stately pace. One of the horses defecated, and a creature similar in type to Fenright scurried out from a hidden place with a bucket and shovel. He began to scoop up the refuse soiling the otherwise immaculate cobblestones, and Marit turned away.

She pressed a button beside the entrance, and a pleasant chiming was heard from within. A moment later, a door opened; revealing a short, stout gentleman with black feathers sprouting from his scalp. He wore servant's livery: a suit of bright-green silk over a pink shirt with a ruffled front.

"Miss Bonderditch." The butler stepped aside, bowing as she passed him to enter the foyer. He closed the door behind her. "Please wait in the public room whilst I fetch Lord Diggersworth."

She went into the formal sitting area and walked across the room to stand near the warm hearth, whose mantel was adorned with photographic portraits in ornate silver frames. Smiling, she studied the faces of the purebred human relations of Lord Diggersworth.

"I can always count on you for perfect punctuality," a voice said.

Marit turned away from the fire and executed a curtsey: not an easy maneuver for a woman whose legs were rarely used. "Your Lordship."

"You may sit if you so desire."

"Thank you, Your Lordship." She went to a chair and seated herself as her host settled down on a couch.

Smiling, she raised her eyes to look at the gentleman. In his fifties, he was tall and thin, with a sunburned face and thick, curly gray hair. He wore a burgundy satin robe that fell almost to his ankles, covering all but the cuffs of his black wool pants.

"Your message indicated that you have something important to discuss," he said. "Would you like to get right to that matter, or shall we discuss the weather?"

"The weather is unremarkable, Your Lordship."

"You don't need to insert my honorific at the end of every statement you make, Marit. Our encounters have been less frequent of late—that much is true—but we've been friends for a long time. Why are you being overly formal?"

"I am not myself today." She stared down at the carpet. "My heart is broken."

"Why?"

"I've discovered an object that can solve the problems of our world. It can restore our depleted natural resources and bring an end to all societal ills." A tear escaped one eye and flowed down her cheek. "I could make this world a paradise for our kind, but I cannot acquire the object!"

"What sort of object can perform a miracle like that?"

"It's a ring that grants wishes. There is no limit to its power."

"I find that difficult to believe."

"An old man was transformed into a youth impervious to injury, aging, and death. I know him, and I know this to be true." She gazed into the man's eyes. "We could have everything we ever wanted. I could make a wish and all the half-breeds would disappear!"

"Who would serve us if they were gone? I don't care for that idea at all."

"I could change the minds of the purebreds pushing for laws that will force us to treat half-breeds as our equals, I suppose."

"Those ridiculous propositions will never be passed into law."

"I could make you young again. You could be immortal!"

"Nice thought, but I do not believe such a ring exists."

"Can you think of any reason why I would lie about such a thing?"

"I cannot, and I know you to be sane, so I'm certain you're not imagining this. It's just that it's quite simply unbelievable."

"Then enable me to prove its existence to you."

"How?"

"The ring is locked in a private storage box inside a bank vault. I can get inside the vault, of course, but I cannot open the box."

"No one can illegally open the private boxes in our banks—it's impossible."

"The bank is in the other world, which has no Goers to threaten the security of vaults. The box has two locks that require two different keys. If I can get past those locks, you will be young forever." Marit leaned forward. "I know you have connections to people with unusual skills. Perhaps you are acquainted with someone who can help us?"

The man paused to think, then nodded. "I know a fellow able to solve this problem. You can transport both the man and his tools?"

"Yes."

"I'll give him a call. First, though …" He smiled. "It's been a while since we had some fun. What do you say?"

"Your wife is not at home this evening?"

"She's away for the holiday week, visiting her relatives in the next county."

Marit rose from her chair, went to the man's side, and put her arms around him. "I say, 'yes.'"

The morning sun streamed in through the big kitchen windows, warming the room. Basker lay before a glass door soaking up the rays as Jennifer stood at the island reading over her shopping list. Verny, perched on her shoulder, perused the list. "I see no mention of tiny mice there."

"You want me to feed you mice?"

"Small little baby ones are best."

"No way! I'll give you raw meat."

"Dead flesh?"

"You eat animals while they're alive?"

"I kill them first, of course, but I like to consume bodies that are warm and fresh."

"Yuck! We're not doing that here. I'll get you something that's been dead a while."

"You are a harsh mistress indeed!"

"I'm not your mistress." She glanced at Baldrick, who was unloading the dishwasher. "Do you know if dragons can survive on old dead stuff?"

"Yes, they can." He pulled a clean plate from the appliance. "I'll wager that Marit never gave him live mice. He's just testing you to see what he can get away with."

"All right! You ended a sentence with a preposition. Thank you for that."

"You're welcome. I do what I must to fit in."

Jennifer folded the shopping list and stuffed it into the back pocket of her jeans. "I should take Verny shopping with me. That would be hilarious! I could cut in at the front of the line at the cash register and no one would say a thing 'cause they'd be terrified."

"If that means I would have to endure being transported in a motorized vehicle, I request that you leave me here."

"I was just joking, Verny." She extended her arm, and the dragon walked down to her elbow and looked at her. "I'm sorry about the mice, little guy. I just can't handle the idea of giving you tiny animals so you can kill them."

"You are forgiven."

"Baldrick, can you dig around in the fridge and see if there's anything Verny might like? I need to be on my way—we're out of cat litter."

"I'll do that right after I rouse Fenright. He sleeps with a determined ferocity, does he not?"

"He does. I'll pick up another bed while I'm out so we can put him in a bedroom where you don't have to listen to his snoring." She headed for the exit. "Bye!"

As she walked towards the garage, she saw Brett strolling up the driveway. "Hi!"

"I'd love it if you'd leave your phone turned on," the man said.

She stopped before the garage door. "I don't like being aggravated by things going off in my purse."

"Did you have a quiet night?"

"Well … Marit showed up with a gun again, and the police said it was loaded this time. Basker restrained her before she could shoot anyone."

"You really should wish for her to disappear, don't you think?"

"I explained the two-key situation for the lockbox to her, so she'll probably leave me alone."

"You're living dangerously. She'll kill you if you don't stop her first!"

Jennifer raised one eyebrow. "Do you think I'm not fit to make my own decisions?"

"You told me you came to this neighborhood because of its excellent security. Being safe is important to you, yet you're unconcerned about a psychopathic woman who pops into your home carrying deadly weapons. The contradiction troubles me."

"I'm not unconcerned, but the idea of using the ring terrifies me more than any threat posed by Marit."

"Why?"

Jennifer paused. "Power like that … it puts me in the position of being a god who doesn't know what she's doing."

"I don't understand."

"It's just … when I made my wish about becoming rich, I asked for cash upfront: ten million dollars that would appear in my bedroom. I laid out all kinds of specifications and guarantees to avoid anything going wrong, but I forgot to say anything about the size of the bills. I ended up with great big piles of small-denomination currency, and it was a pain in the neck dealing with it. I realize that's not a big deal, but it proves that things can and probably will go wrong if I make a mistake."

"Your life's at risk! How can any bad side effect of wishing be worse than being murdered?"

Jennifer bit her lower lip. "Watching the world fall into chaos because I made a mistake would be worse."

Brett threw up his hands. "All right! Go ahead and let her kill you!"

"Lighten up. She ain't gonna kill me."

The man sighed.

"This conversation is going nowhere, and I gotta go buy litter before the cats start pooping on the floor." Jennifer smiled. "If you have time, go inside and meet my new roommates."

"Did you get some more animals?"

"Not exactly. Go in and say hi. I gotta get outta here." She turned away and headed for the garage. "Bye!"

Chapter 8

Marit stood in Lord Diggersworth's foyer. "Are you ready to go, Mr. Hart?"

Mr. Hart, a muscular fellow of medium height whose facial features were obscured by short brown fur, nodded. "Yes. I'm a little nervous, I must admit. I've never traveled with a Goer."

"It's a simple process, and you won't feel a thing." She smiled. "Get a good strong grip on your toolbox."

He leaned down and picked it up. "I'm ready!"

She took his hand. "We'll be back soon, Your Lordship."

"I'll be here. Good luck!"

It wasn't easy transporting both the man and his toolbox, but the determined woman managed it, and they found themselves inside the bank vault.

"Oh!" Mr. Hart said. "I didn't expect it to happen so quickly."

"We must move with haste, sir. There are survey cameras about, and law enforcement will be alerted to our presence."

"Which one is it?"

She pointed to Jennifer's box. Mr. Hart went to it and stared at the keyholes. "Hm … I'm guessing that the two required keys wouldn't need to be engaged simultaneously. If one lock needs to be opened before the other, well … we'll find out, won't we?"

"Hurry!"

"Don't rush me." He took a few slow, deep breaths in and out. "All right," he whispered. Turning, he shot a look at Marit. "Give me some space!"

She backed away and watched, wringing her hands and trembling, as the half-breed used his tools to manipulate the locks. In a short time, a sliding sound followed by a clicking noise indicated success.

He opened the brass door and pulled out a metal box. "I can take care of this in no time." He defeated the unimpressive lock on the container in an instant and handed it to Marit. "Here you are, ma'am."

She hesitated. "I can't believe I have it!"

"What's in there?"

"Just a piece of jewelry I fancy." She smiled and lifted the lid. "No. No. No, no, no!" She threw the box across the chamber.

Squirming a bit, Mr. Hart looked up at the ceiling. "Can we get out of here, please?"

Marit opened her mouth and wailed like a proper banshee.

"I would like to go now!" He put away his tools.

The wailing continued.

He picked up his toolbox, went to the woman, and grabbed her wrist. "If you don't calm down and get us out of here, I'll get violent. I'm a criminal, you know!"

"Yes, sir." Forcing herself to return to an acceptable level of sanity, she closed her eyes and concentrated.

The pair appeared in Lord Diggersworth's public room. The gentleman was in a chair reading a magazine, and looked up. "You have it!" He rose to his feet. "Show me!"

"She has nothing," Mr. Hart said. "She threw the box across the room and yelled like a lunatic, so I'm assuming it was empty."

"Is this true?"

"It's a minor problem," Marit replied. "The woman moved it to a different hiding place. I'll find it."

"I'd appreciate being paid now. I did what was required."

Lord Diggersworth pulled a small sack from an inside pocket of his jacket and handed it to Mr. Hart. "I appreciate your efficiency. Good evening."

The half-breed left the room.

"Do you want to know how much I had to pay him for what amounts to nothing? You owe me, Marit!"

"How could I have known the ring was moved?"

"You and your imaginary ring … I was an idiot to have trusted you. Get out!"

Marit began to walk towards the foyer.

"You'd better get out faster than that!"

Stopping, she closed her eyes and concentrated. Seeing her fail to dematerialize, the man pushed the stumbling woman all the way to the front door and out onto the porch.

As the door slammed shut behind her, she fell to her knees on the marble pavement. A carriage passed by in the darkness; its lanterns illuminating the driver's face as he stared at Marit.

She rose to her feet before anyone else could see her and descended the stairs. On the sidewalk, she dug in her handbag, pulled out a money sack, and counted the coins. 'Just enough to buy a ride home, if I can make it to the public street.'

She trudged ahead; the cement sidewalk scraping the soles of her bare feet as she headed for the low-rent part of town.

AFTER JENNIFER unloaded all her purchases from her car, she went into the front room. Brett was seated on the floor; leaning back against a wall as he watched the dragon flit about before him.

"There was no need for smelling salts this time," Baldrick said.

"I'm glad to hear that." She turned to Fenright, who was crouching on the bed. "There's an inflatable bed in a package in the kitchen. If you'd like to choose a bedroom and set it up, you won't have to deal with Baldrick poking you during the night."

"Thank you." The halfling scurried away.

Basker appeared. He went to Jennifer's side, and she stroked his head. "Everyone getting along all right?"

"I think so." Brett stopped watching the dragon and smiled at the woman. "I believe I'm getting used to encountering alien forms."

A telephone rang in a distant room. "Excuse me!" She trotted to her office and answered the phone. "Hello?"

"Ms. Grace?"

"Yes."

"Ms. Parker here."

"Hi! How are you?"

The bank manager sighed. "Your friend was in the vault again."

"She's not my friend." Jennifer sank into her desk chair.

"Well, yes. I just ..." Ms. Parker sighed again. "She broke into one of your safe-deposit boxes. To be more precise, a man who was with her picked the locks."

"I'm really sorry to hear that."

"Even though it appears that nothing was taken, I felt you should know about this. Our video shows her throwing the box against a wall and screaming, so I'm assuming whatever it is that she wanted wasn't in there."

"I moved it to another box right after you and I met."

"You might consider finding a different place to store your valuables."

"Are you telling me to take my business elsewhere?"

"No, I'm not. We value your patronage." Ms. Parker cleared her throat. "It's just that, with the means you have at your disposal, you should be able to come up with some sort of security system that can thwart this woman's attempts; maybe a setup with live guards on duty twenty-four hours a day."

Jennifer paused. "The last job I had was working as a stable manager. I don't know anything about how to repel thieves."

"I see."

"I'm grateful that you called. I'll consider what you've said."

"Thank you, Ms. Grace."

"Goodbye, Ms. Parker." She hung up the phone.

Brett entered the office. "So, you do have a phone that rings once in a while!"

"That's for business stuff." Jennifer leaned forward, putting her elbows on the desk, and covered her face with both hands.

"Bad news?"

She uncovered her face. "Marit returned to the vault and got into one of my lockboxes: the empty one, fortunately."

"Oh."

"I think I need to hire a private army."

"Not an entirely bad idea, I suppose."

"I'm kinda stressed and my brain isn't working too well right now."

"Do you want to be alone?"

"Yes, please."

"Okay, I'll see you later." He left the room.

Jennifer spun her chair around and stared out the window. 'I could destroy the ring or throw it in the ocean,' she thought, 'but Marit wouldn't believe it was gone and she'd end up killing me and everyone in this house.' She watched as a breeze blew through the trees at the back of the property, sending their boughs waving back and forth. 'This is a nightmare.'

She turned her chair back to the desk. 'I need to talk to a cold-blooded person who knows how to survive.' Picking up her phone, she called Linda.

The housekeeper answered. "De Kuyper residence."

"Hello, Anita. This is Jennifer Grace."

"Hi! How are you?"

"I'm doing okay, thank you. How are you?"

"Fine."

"Can I speak to Mrs. De Kuyper?"

"Let me see if she's available."

She waited, and heard another line pick up. "Hello, Jennifer."

"Hello, Linda."

"I never thought I'd hear from you again." She chuckled. "I understand your fortunes have changed."

"Yes, that's why I called. Someone wants something valuable that I own and she won't leave me alone; in fact, she keeps coming into my house and threatening me with guns."

"Whoa! What do the police have to say about this?"

"They are unable to assist me in this matter."

"Stopping lunatics can be problematic at best. Do you own a gun?"

"I don't, and I don't know how to handle one. I need an immediate solution that doesn't require learning a new skill."

"You need a bodyguard. I can give you an executive-protection agency's number. Hang on."

"Wait a sec. I … I was rude to you the last time we spoke. I'm sorry about that; I'm just not suited to being a servant. You got me off the streets, and I should've been more grateful."

"I didn't make things easy for you, I suppose."

"It was a difficult job."

"I'll get you that number. Hang on."

Linda returned to the phone and read out the number. Jennifer paused for a moment. "Is this firm good about keeping secrets?"

"Oh, yes; they're complete professionals."

"Great. I have some unusual roommates, and I'd rather no one broadcasted the details of their identities."

"We'll have to have lunch sometime, and you can tell me all about them."

"Yeah." Jennifer paused. "I assume you have the number on hand because you used the services of this agency. Why did you need a bodyguard?"

"I'd rather not talk about it."

"Okay. Thanks, Linda."

"You're welcome."

Jennifer hung up the phone. Boris appeared and jumped up onto her lap. "Think we're gonna need smelling salts for my bodyguard, sweetie?" She shook her head. "This is gonna be weird." She tapped at her keyboard to wake up the computer. "Before I call, let's see if I can get a ballistic vest for Basker." A quick check revealed that such garments weren't sold to anyone outside the law-enforcement field. "Okay, I'll just have to keep him out of my bedroom at night, since that's where Marit always shows up. Same for you and Natasha."

She called the security firm and made the arrangements, then sent an email to Brett to let him know she was being protected.

Shortly before dark, the obnoxious bell rang. Jennifer opened the door: three unusually large and beefy men in ill-fitting suits stood before her.

"Oh!" she said. "You're all so big!"

One man smiled, but the other two retained their ultra-serious expressions.

"Before you guys come in, I need to explain something." She stepped out onto the porch and closed the door. "I have three roommates who're kinda unusual."

"We can handle unusual people," one man said.

"They aren't exactly people."

"Animals?"

"Well ..." Jennifer made a little groaning noise. "Uh ..."

"I need to check the perimeter," a man said.

"You'd be wasting your time doing that. The intruder won't be hanging out in the yard or creeping around the building."

"How do you know that, ma'am?"

She closed her eyes. "Okay."

"Okay what?"

She looked at the men. "You won't believe anything I need to tell you until you go inside and meet my roomies. Most important thing you need to know: my friends aren't dangerous. Don't go shooting them just 'cause they scare you, all right?"

"We're trained in risk assessment and not about to randomly shoot innocent people."

"Like I said, they're not people." Jennifer smiled. "One of them is a dragon."

Six eyes rolled heavenward.

"Come inside." They followed her into the foyer. "Stop here." She turned and looked at them. "Do not shoot!" She turned around, took a breath, then shouted, "Baldrick!"

The bird-man trotted into view. "Yes, Jennifer?"

"Verny!"

The dragon emerged from a corridor and flew to the woman's shoulder.

"Fenright!"

"He's sleeping," Baldrick said.

Verny checked out the men standing behind Jennifer. "You fellows look a bit stiff."

She walked forward and descended the steps leading to the living room. Turning around, she looked at the frozen trio of security agents. "You're doing fine, gentlemen."

The dragon flew into the air and hovered before the bodyguards, looking closely at each expressionless face before moving on to the next.

"Stop tormenting them, Verny," Baldrick said. "You're being unkind."

He whipped around and returned to Jennifer's shoulder.

"May I serve you gentlemen some tea? My magnificent silver pot arrived today, and I'm so very anxious to use it." The bird-man grinned. "Please?"

"Tea," a man said.

"There are fresh-baked cookies to go with the tea."

"Tea and cookies."

"We're in Wonderland, men. Let's go with it." The agent in the middle of the trio stepped forward. "I'll have some tea; thank you."

"Excellent! Follow me, please."

Jennifer crawled under the bedcovers. Sitting up, she smiled at the two bodyguards seated in opposing corners of the room. "Should I leave the light on?"

"A soft light would be helpful," Stephen said.

"I have a night light. I'll turn it on."

"I'll do that. Where is it located?" John rose from his chair.

"In that corner." Jennifer pointed, and he went to it and switched it on. She turned off the bedside light and put her head on the pillow. "Thank you for tolerating my bizarre situation. I really didn't want to ask for outside help, but that woman will kill me and everyone in my house if she isn't stopped."

"We understand, Miss Grace." Stephen nodded. "Rest assured: she will be stopped."

"She usually appears at the foot of my bed and …"

"There's no need for you to repeat yourself. I know you feel vulnerable, but we have the matter well in hand. Go to sleep."

"Thank you, John." Jennifer closed her eyes for a moment, then raised her head again. "You're sure your vests will protect you?"

"Yes, ma'am. Go to sleep."

The sound of gunshots woke her. "No!" She sat up; heart racing.

Marit lay on the floor; a pistol at her side. John stood over her. Kneeling, he felt the side of her throat. He spoke into his radio. "Armed intruder down. No pulse detected."

Thundering footsteps came up the stairs. As the third agent ran into the room, Marit vanished.

Jennifer collapsed onto her back. "Was she dead?"

Baldrick appeared. "Did they get her?"

"She had no pulse," John said.

"Yet she is gone."

"Do Goers disappear when they die?" Jennifer got up and stood next to the bed.

"They do not."

"I shot her in the heart," Stephen said.

"So did I."

"Exactly where is your heart?" Baldrick asked.

John pointed to the area on his torso.

"Hers is located quite a bit to the right of that."

"Someone should've told us that."

"I'm sorry; I didn't know your hearts are in a different place."

Fenright scrambled into the room. "What's going on?"

"They shot Marit twice but missed her heart."

"She had no pulse!" John shook his head. "No pulse at all." He looked at Fenright. "Where's the main artery to the head in people like her?"

"At the back of our necks. Do you want to feel mine?"

"I'll take your word for it, thank you."

"She's getting to be awfully good at transporting herself during periods of stress," Jennifer said.

"I expect she's been practicing that particular skill." Baldrick looked at the pistol, then at the woman. "Maybe you should hang onto that so you can fight back the next time she returns."

"Maybe she'll die from her wounds? I can hope for that."

"Most likely, she transported herself straight to one of our hospitals."

"This sucks so incredibly much!" Jennifer plopped down on the floor. "I thought if I hit her with enough opposition, she'd give up, but nothing scares her off; not even the hound of the Baskervilles holding her down and growling into her face. She's insane. How do I fight back against an insane person?"

"You'll have some time before she recovers. You people don't have an absurd immunity to wounds, right?" Stephen glared at Fenright.

"I don't know how we compare to folks like you, but two bullets in Marit's upper torso will result in surgery and a long stretch of bed rest."

Baldrick went to Jennifer and stroked the top of her head. "You should recover from all this stress before making any more decisions."

"No point in putting things off." She closed her eyes and leaned back against the bed. "It's time to use the big guns. I'll go to the bank tomorrow."

Jennifer opened her safe-deposit compartment and withdrew the ring box. She put the gold band on her finger, trembling as the metal pulsed against her flesh. Reading from a scrap of paper, she said, "This is what I wish for: Marit will never again set foot in my world. This is my wish." She removed the ring and locked it away.

Chapter 9

Jennifer sat cross-legged on the grass, listening to the pleasant gurgling of her new waterfall. Above her head, Verny zoomed about the sunlit garden; keeping his eyes on the ground in hope of locating tiny rodents.

"If you catch any mice, please don't tell me about it."

"I can keep the exciting tales of my victorious mouse captures to myself, but you might hear some shrieking when I kill them."

Jennifer shuddered.

"Hey!"

She turned; Ryan was coming down the steps at the back of the house. "Hey! Come and sit beside my new pond!"

He settled down next to her. "Is that thing flying around up there the dragon you told me about?"

"Verny's hunting mice. I decided to stop being paranoid about people seeing my strange friends in my yard, and he's making the most of his freedom. I don't know why I felt like I had to hide everyone; it's not as though their presence is illegal or anything. Besides, with this huge lot of mine, no one can see into my yard unless they're trespassing."

"Hi, Verny!" Ryan waved as the creature soared over the pond. "I have to tell you; I'm so glad you decided to use a wish to keep Marit at bay. I was worried about you."

"Thanks. It's been a couple of weeks now, and I'm finally starting to feel secure again." She uncrossed her legs and lay back on the grass. "Using that ring scared me; it's … it's just so much power! And I don't know where it came from or what the source of the power is or what kind of intelligence is behind it all: it's terrifying."

"I tried not to think about that. The man who gave it to me didn't know anything about it, and the woman who gave it to him didn't have a clue, and so on."

"Well … it can't be very old, since the formula the note says to recite is in modern English."

"Right, and if you change one word of it, the wish won't work, so it's not a translation from an ancient language. The intent of the formula isn't what's important: it's the words themselves."

Jennifer waved at the dragon. "Let's go inside and have lunch, Verny!" She rose to her feet. "Baldrick is really excited about having a fabulous new dining table—he's been cooking all morning so he can cover it with food and the antique silver I bought for him.

He's so domestic; not to mention kind and thoughtful as well."

"The perfect roommate for you, I imagine," Ryan said.

"I hope he never decides to go back home. I'd miss him."

They went into the house and admired the display of food, fancy dishes, and cut flowers atop the new table.

"Please be seated," Baldrick said.

Standing before her mirror, Marit fussed with the low neckline of her emerald-green gown to see if the stitched-up incisions in her flesh would be revealed if she moved about in a normal fashion. They didn't show. Smiling at her reflection, she disappeared from the room.

She reappeared before the front door of a large white house. Its outward appearance was similar to the gingerbread Victorians of our world, but over the windows, panels of lead shielded passersby from the home's inhabitant.

Marit stood in the bright sunlight, eyes closed, as she concentrated on fighting off her fear. Pressing a button, she heard a buzzing sound go off inside the house.

"Hello!" shouted a voice inside the dwelling.

"It's Miss Bonderditch!"

"I can't open the door, you know! Come inside your own way!"

Marit transported herself into the foyer. Before her stood a young man in a red satin frock coat and green velvet trousers. His black beard, its generous length obscuring the blue-silk cravat about his throat, was well-groomed and adorned with numerous pearls.

He bowed. "Miss Bonderditch … you honor my humble home with your presence."

"It is I who am honored, Mr. Frinkland." She entered the house, fighting to control the trembling of her limbs.

"I've set out some pastries and whatnot in the parlor. Would you care to partake of them?"

"You set them out yourself? Has something happened to your servant?"

The young man smiled and tilted his head to one side. "There was a tiny mishap, and she is no longer with us."

Marit swallowed hard.

"It was a quick death, and Louisa did not suffer … much."

She nodded; staring at the floor.

"Don't be concerned about yourself. The event released most of the excess energy from my system, so I'll not likely go off again—inadvertently, that is—for at least a week."

She tried to smile, but the resulting expression was just plain ghastly.

"Come into the parlor, please."

They left the dark entry area and entered a sitting room illuminated by numerous candles. Mr. Frinkland offered Marit a chair. She sat, and he pushed a wheeled cart laden with small cakes and sandwiches to her side.

"I recommend the seafood with white paste … these triangular bits here." He pointed to a plate, and Marit picked up one of the tiny sandwiches.

She put the entire thing into her mouth and swallowed; forgetting to chew first. Her eyes bulged as she leaned forward, honking up the mouthful of food. "Excuse me!" Grabbing a napkin from the cart, she wiped her chin and lap.

Giggling, Mr. Frinkland took a seat near the cart. He selected a chocolate tidbit and tossed it into the air. As it began to fall, he pointed at it with one finger. The sweet hung motionless in the air for a few seconds, then movements of the man's finger guided the bit of food slowly down and into his open mouth. Marit watched this process, then chose another sandwich; remembering to chew this time.

"So …" the young man said, "what has led you to challenge death by visiting my little abode?"

"You're the most powerful man I know, and I need your help."

After the lunch feast, Jennifer went into her office, sat before the computer, and opened a browser. Ryan, seated in a chair beside her, leaned forward to watch. She went to a charity's website, entered a '1' followed by many zeroes into a box, and followed up with her debit-card information. She hit the 'donate' button and let out a whoop.

"Feels great, doesn't it?"

"Yeah!" She settled back in her chair. "These people have enough smarts to run homeless shelters that don't need scary signs posted on the walls."

Ryan held up his hand.

"What?"

"High five!"

"Oh, dear," she said. "I don't know how to do that; you'll have to teach me."

"You really are a hermit, aren't you?"

"Books are my best friends. They don't turn on me, and if they let me down, I can throw them against the wall."

"Can't say that much for people. Throw 'em against the wall and you'd be in big trouble."

"Yeah." She touched Ryan's arm. "I'm sorry to bring this up again, but I keep worrying about you and your living-forever business. I mean, well … for one thing, no matter how much money you wished for, it can't be enough to last forever."

"I invested in real estate. I'll be okay."

"But what if …"

"I gave myself a way out. If, for example, a gigantic meteor hits the planet and it turns into a wasteland, I can choose to turn off the immortality stuff. Don't worry."

"That's a big relief!"

Basker trotted into the room; Boris at his side. The dog lay on the floor beside Jennifer's feet, and the kitten curled up next to his belly.

"I think I should get a big doggy friend for Basker so they can play together in the yard. Want to go to the shelter with me?"

"Sure!"

As the pair started to rise from their chairs, the wolfhound raised his head, then jumped to his feet. Running to the window, he stood looking out and growling.

"What is it, Basker?" Jennifer went to the window, but saw nothing. "I'll be right back." She ran out of the room, returning with a pair of binoculars. Focusing on the trees at the back of the property, she took in a deep breath. "Oh, no." She set the glasses on the desk and fell into her chair. "Marit's here. There's a man with her."

"That isn't possible."

"She's here."

"What did you say when you wished for her to stay away?"

"Uh … 'Marit will never again set foot in my world.'"

"You didn't use her last name?"

"I didn't know she had one."

"Still … that should've ensured that everyone named Marit would disappear from the planet."

"What? It never occurred to me that anyone else would have that name!"

"It's not terribly uncommon for women in certain countries."

"What have I done? Did women all over the world cease to exist? What have I done?"

"Don't panic. If your wish had worked exactly as stated, she wouldn't be here."

"I wrote down the entire statement while I was home. The wish formula is in the lockbox with the ring, so I didn't copy from that. I must've done it wrong. Wait here." She ran out of the office. A few minutes later, she entered the room holding a scrap of paper. "I saved this in my memory box. I don't see anything wrong with it!" She handed it to Ryan.

He read the words. "You used 'this' instead of 'that' in your closing statement."

"I'm an idiot!"

"It's an easy mistake to make when you're totally stressed out, I suppose. Look on the bright side: if you'd said 'that' instead of 'this,' you'd be responsible for the disappearance of thousands of women."

"Okay; there's a bright side. I'm not feeling it!" She went back to the window and used the glasses to look at the two intruders. "I wonder who that man is?"

"What's all the shouting about?" Baldrick appeared in the doorway.

"I screwed up, and Marit's returned. There's a man with her."

"Maybe it's someone I know. May I use the scopes?"

Jennifer handed him the binoculars.

Baldrick looked at the pair lurking in the trees and gasped. Dropping the glasses to the floor, he backed away from the window and hid behind the desk. "It's the Malvole!"

"Please explain," Jennifer said.

"I've never seen the man before—only photographs—but that's him." Baldrick tightened his trembling body into a ball of quivering feathers. "He's the most dangerous creature in our world. He can kill with a thought and move objects without touching them. He can get inside a person's mind and twist their desires to match his own. He's a monster!"

Ryan picked up the glasses and went to the window. "Marit has a strange expression on her face."

"She's insane to try to form an alliance with the Malvole. As soon as he doesn't need her anymore, she'll be dead. What does she think … he'll help her get the ring and let her keep it? That's absurd!"

"Maybe she thinks he's a sucker for a good-looking woman."

"Her outrageous conceit might have led her to believe she can use him, but she's wrong."

"Is there no defense against him?" Jennifer asked.

"His powers cannot pass through lead."

"That's no good right now. There must be some other way to control him, otherwise he'd be ruling your world, right?"

The bird-man raised his head. "Fenright!"

Moments later, the halfling scampered into the room. "You summoned me, Baldrick?"

"The Malvole is here."

"Oh, that's not good."

"An understatement, Fenright. Perhaps you know more about him than I. Does he have a weakness we can use to defend ourselves against him?"

"You could always go back home; you'd be safe there."

"I'm not abandoning Jennifer."

"Thank you!" she said.

"Think, Fenright. How does our government keep him from using his powers?"

"I don't know." He went to the doorway. "Verny!"

The dragon flew into view. "What's going on?"

"The Malvole is here."

"We're in trouble!" He landed on the back of a chair. Lowering his head, he folded his wings over it.

"Do you know how our government keeps this guy in line?"

"In line?" He put his wings down against his body. "Good question there!"

"We need an internet connection to the other world," Ryan said.

"We're doomed for sure!" Baldrick's head bobbed up and down.

"He can't kill or even hurt me. I could go out there and deal with him."

"Your body is invincible, but what about your mind? He can get inside it and turn you against us."

"I need a lead helmet. Where can I get one?" He sat down at Jennifer's computer and began a search. "Okay, here's one: 'How to build a post-apocalyptic helmet.' Don't really have time for that. Maybe one of those blankets that are put on before getting x-rays?" He searched further. "Um … ships in two weeks."

"Even if you had one of those right now, you wouldn't be able to deal with anyone, much less this Malvole thing, with a lead blanket stuck on your head." Jennifer began to pace the room, then stopped. "They've been out there for a few minutes at least. Why haven't they swooped on in here so that creature can capture my brain?" Basker continued to stand at the window and growl; his nose touching the glass. "Calm down, boy." She stroked his head. "All we can do is make a run for it. Where can I take all my animals and weird friends?"

"My house?"

"Marit knows where that is, I expect."

"Yeah. Oh, I know! I have a cabin she wouldn't know about. It's remote but not too far away. Here's the address." He grabbed pen and paper from the desk and wrote it down. "I have to go home to get the keys to it. I'll see you there in less than an hour." He ran from the room.

Jennifer looked over the assembly. "My car doesn't have seating for everybody, and I'm not putting my animals in the trunk. Baldrick and Fenright: you'll need to hunker down on the floor in the back. Verny can perch between the two cat carriers."

"What's hunker down?" the halfling asked.

"Crouch down low. I don't want anyone seeing you if I can help it; we have enough to worry about."

"I'll put the cats into their carriers." Fenright scampered off.

"I have to grab the keys to my lockbox. You guys wait here with Basker."

Baldrick and Verny huddled before the desk—the wolfhound still at the window growling—until Jennifer appeared in the doorway with Fenright and the cats. "Help Fenright carry the cats, Baldrick." She put a leash on Basker and led him outside.

As the group hurried from the house towards the garage, Jennifer saw Ophelia standing in the driveway. Her mouth was open, and there was a letter on the ground beside her.

"Hey, Ophelia! What's up?"

There was no response from the cook, who stood staring.

Jennifer handed Basker's leash to Fenright and ran to the woman; followed by the airborne dragon. "We have to get out of here. Do you need something?"

"Your mail … delivered to us."

"Thanks." She picked up the letter Ophelia had dropped and stuffed it into a pocket. "Can't explain; no time. Get out of here quick; as in right now! This place is dangerous."

The cook was fast on her feet; there was no doubt about that.

RYAN PARKED his Mercedes in the garage. He opened the door leading into his house and stopped.

Marit smiled. "I'd like to introduce you to Mr. Frinkland."

Chapter 10

Jennifer sat in the car with her friends, looking at their temporary refuge. What Ryan had referred to as a 'cabin' was actually a Pacific-Lodge-style mansion. The rear portion of the building was earth-sheltered —buried under a manmade hill planted with wildflowers and small bushes—which made it impossible to ascertain the true size of the timbered structure.

The coniferous forest surrounding the retreat sent a pleasant fragrance into the car's open windows; soothing the visitors. The nearest neighbors were miles away, and the area was free of the sounds of human civilization. Insects buzzed, and a few birds chirped, but the place was otherwise silent.

"This is nice," Verny said. "There will be lots of mice here for me to capture!"

Jennifer glanced at her watch. "Ryan should be here soon." She pulled her phone from her purse and checked for messages; finding a rather intense communication from Brett. "Guess I better call him back." She did so, and waited for him to answer. "Hi. Is Ophelia okay?" Biting her lower lip, she squirmed in her seat as she listened to his description of events. "Sorry … I didn't have much choice. The usual villain showed up with an even worse villain. We didn't have time to be sneaky while we made a run for it." She nodded. "Uh, huh. It didn't work." Looking out the window, she watched a squirrel scurry up a tree trunk. "We've got a safe place to stay. Whatever you do, don't go onto my property, even if the house catches fire or something. You might get killed. I gotta go. Bye!"

"I'm getting cramps in my legs," Fenright said. "May I disembark from this vehicle, please?"

"Oh, sorry! Sure … both you guys can get out and walk around; just stay where I can see you so I won't worry."

"May I take Basker with me?"

"Uh, huh. Don't let go of his leash if something gets him excited. I don't know what kind of wild animals live here, but I don't want him killing any of them. His hunting instinct is strong, and if he sees moving prey, he'll go for it."

Fenright and Baldrick climbed out; taking the wolfhound with them. Jennifer watched as they walked up the gentle incline of the driveway to the house and peered into a ground-level window. She opened her car door and stepped onto the asphalt pavement. "Don't touch the glass! There's probably a security system and you don't want to set it off."

Baldrick grinned and waved, and the pair stepped back from the window.

Jennifer heard an approaching car, and turned to see Ryan driving up. He parked behind her and left the vehicle.

"Did you have any trouble finding the place?"

"No, I …" Hearing a low growl, she turned around to look at Basker. "What's wrong, boy?"

Fenright was being dragged forward by the wolfhound, who was attempting to break into a run. Baldrick added his hands to the long leash, which resulted in both of the lightweight creatures being pulled towards thc parked cars by the snarling canine.

Verny emerged from Jennifer's vehicle and floated above the moving trio; looking down in fascination. "He wants to kill something!"

"Whoa, Basker!" She tossed her head. "I'm an idiot; he's not a horse." She jumped in front of the dog. "Settle!"

The wolfhound stopped. Standing in place, he tilted his head to one side; eyeballing Ryan and snarling. Jennifer stepped aside as she turned to look at the man. The dog broke free from his handlers and leapt onto the cause of his rage, knocking him onto his back.

"Release!" Jennifer panicked when the gigantic dog ignored the command. "Release, release, release!"

Baldrick, Fenright, and the woman ran to the wolfhound and grabbed his leash. Between the three of them, they managed to pull him off Ryan. "Help me get him in the car!" They managed to pull him to the side of the vehicle, but getting the furious and very strong animal into it was another matter: one which proved impossible.

Jennifer wanted to cry, but held back. "Why in the hell does he hate you all of a sudden?" she shouted.

Ryan sat up and pulled a gun from a jacket pocket. He stared at it for a moment, then threw it into the bushes at the side of pavement. "Basker—I'm sorry!"

The wolfhound relaxed; once more his usual gentle self.

Jennifer let go of the leash. Sliding down against the side of the car, she sat on the ground; head lowered. Fenright opened one of the doors. "Inside, Basker." The dog entered the vehicle; settling down on the floor in front of the cat-filled back seat. The halfling shut the door.

Ryan got up onto his feet. "Marit was waiting for me at my house and introduced me to the Malvole. He got inside my head, but I'm okay now."

Jennifer's breathing returned to normal. "I'll take Basker's word for it that you're yourself again." She looked at Ryan. "What's with the gun? Were you going to kill me?"

"Marit gave it to me and told me to shoot Basker. Mr. Frinkland—the Malvole—has a problem with animals. They tend to hate him on sight, and he can't kill or control them."

"I didn't know that," Baldrick said. "If he's afraid of Basker, we have a chance of survival."

"Yes."

"It's going to take me a while to recover from losing control of him. That was terrifying!" Jennifer sucked in a deep breath. "You know, wolfhounds used to go into battle and pull men off horses and chariots. I can totally see Basker doing that."

"I didn't fully realize how big he is until he was on top of me."

"Are you all right?"

"I had the wind knocked out of me, but you know: immortality and all that."

"I forgot about it! I could've let him chew on you and it wouldn't have mattered; you would've healed up like a vampire or something."

"Let's not test that theory." Ryan adjusted his ponytail and brushed the driveway's dirt off his backside. "I can feel pain, you know."

"What would happen if someone chopped off your head? Would it roll back onto your shoulders and reattach itself?"

"I don't know, and I don't want to find out."

"Okay." Jennifer nodded. "I need to get Boris and Natasha out of those carriers—they hate 'em. Can we go inside?"

"Sure." Ryan pulled the keys from his pocket. "I should mention that Marit and her friend now know where we are. I'm sorry about that."

"You had no choice in the matter." She got up off the ground. "Basker will protect us from them … but maybe you should dig that gun out of the bushes just in case we need a little extra help." She glanced around at the forest. "This place is no safer for us than my home, but the lack of neighbors close by will prevent collateral damage to the public. We should stay here until this matter is resolved, if that's okay with you."

"That's fine."

Once everyone was inside the house, the cat carriers were set down. "I don't think letting them have the run of this huge place is a good idea," she said. "If there's trouble, I want to be able to catch them quickly."

"We should all stay together in one room for safety. I have a large bedroom upstairs with two beds. I'll show you where it is, and you can let the cats loose."

The pair headed for the wide staircase; each human carrying a caged feline. "Come along with us, guys," Jennifer said, "and bring Basker."

The trio of other-world creatures, preceded by the dog, climbed the stairs and followed the humans to the bedroom. Baldrick closed the door when all were inside, and the cats were released from their containers. It took no time at all for them to disappear under a bed.

"Every little thing we have to do now is going to be really complicated." Jennifer sighed. "Do you have anything I can use for a litter box? We can fill it with dirt for now."

"I have a plastic storage box that'll do the job."

"I didn't bring any pet food. Crap! How can we accomplish simple things like shopping when we have to stay together in a pack so Basker can protect us?"

She fell into a chair and closed her eyes; scrunching up her face like someone in physical pain.

"Don't think about dealing with all the problems right now. We have some time before we have to worry about Marit and the Malvole showing up. I promised to call them when Basker was dead, so they'll be waiting for me to do that."

"Are they carrying cell phones?"

"No, they're at my house waiting for the call to come in through my landline."

"Okay, I can relax a tiny bit for a little while, then."

"I keep basic food here, so don't worry about that. There's lots of canned stuff and nonperishables like flour and sugar."

"I can bake," Baldrick said.

Jennifer looked at the bird-man. "I think … things would be easier if you weren't here."

"Oh." He stared down at the floor.

"That didn't come out right. You know I adore you, Baldrick. It's just … if I didn't have to worry about you and Verny and Fenright getting killed, the situation would be simpler."

"If you went back home," Ryan said, "you could gather information about the Malvole. When you've learned something that can help us eliminate him as a threat, you can come back."

Baldrick grinned. "I can do that!"

"I don't want to go back there. I have nowhere to sleep and no way to buy food." Fenright addressed the dragon. "Do you want to go back?"

"Nope." Verny left the table he'd perched on and floated into the center of the big room. "I don't want to go!"

"You're an animal, aren't you?" Jennifer asked. "Maybe the Malvole can't hurt you."

"I have a bit of human in me: that's why I can talk." He dipped down and landed on a bed.

"Then you'd better leave."

"My family won't let you two starve," Baldrick said. "And as long as we don't stay for an extended period of time, they'll let you sleep in their home."

"It's settled—you're leaving." She left her seat and kissed the two larger creatures on their cheeks. "Give me a love peck, Verny." He flew onto her outstretched arm and bumped his face against her nose. "I'm going to miss you all, but this is the best way to proceed."

The dragon flew to Baldrick's shoulder. Fenright held onto the bird-man's hand, and the trio disappeared.

Jennifer fell back into her chair. "I'm afraid I'll never see them again!" Leaning forward, she grabbed a handful of her long hair and began to twist it around her fingers.

"Don't go tearing your hair out. Maybe if we go to the store and get pet supplies, the activity …" He shook his head. "It won't make much difference in how we feel, but if the animals are fed, that's one less thing to worry about."

"Marit and her monster might show up while we're gone with Basker, and she'll kill my cats just for the fun of it."

"I don't think they'll be coming here anytime soon, but …" He paused. "I have a secret room we can put them in. Marit won't know the cats are there, so she can't hurt them."

"I don't know if I like that idea."

"There's a pet store ten minutes from here. We can get the supplies and be back in less than half an hour."

"Well …" Jennifer chewed at one of her fingertips. "The likelihood of the monsters showing up increases with every passing minute, so we better do it now."

After much coaxing, the felines came out from under the bed and allowed themselves to be put into their carriers. Jennifer picked up Natasha's box. "Come on, Basker."

Ryan took Boris, and the group went downstairs. The man led the woman and dog through a doorway and switched on a light. Inside the big room, a group of chairs faced a huge television, and a pool table sat in a corner.

"Watch closely," Ryan said. "I'll show you how to open this."

She followed him to a tall wooden rack set in a wall near the pool table. It held an assortment of cues and small blocks of blue chalk; at the top hung the triangle used to set up the balls at the beginning of games.

"Feel here." He pointed to a recessed area behind the molding around the rack's outer edge. She put her fingers in the indicated area and felt a large metal button. "Push that."

She pressed the button, and the rack jumped out two inches from the wall. Ryan went to its right side and pulled, and it swung open like a door; revealing a an empty room about ten feet square. "That's interesting. What's it for?"

"Hiding stuff, I suppose. I didn't ask the previous owner why he had it put in here."

"The cats will be comfortable in there … it has thick carpeting. All they need is a big bowl of water."

"I'll get that." Ryan jogged out of the room.

Jennifer moved the cats into the chamber. When Ryan returned with the bowl of water, she unlatched the carrier doors but didn't open them. The humans retreated; putting the cue rack back in place before the felines realized they could get out of their boxes.

"Okay! Now it's just you, me, and the mighty hound." She ran one hand through her hair. "Um … did Marit and the Malvole expect you to, uh, kill Basker right away?"

"It wasn't discussed. She handed me the gun and told me to kill him and then call to let them know it was done. I didn't say anything; I just went back to my car and drove here."

"How did it feel to have that thing controlling your mind?"

"Oddly enough, it felt perfectly normal. I thought murdering a dog was a fine thing to do. I wasn't even aware that I was under his control until Basker knocked me down and the physical shock brought me back to myself."

"That's horrible!"

'Yeah, well … we'd better get going. Pet stores usually let people take their animals inside, don't they?"

"If your local one doesn't, I'll bribe 'em to overlook Basker's presence."

"Your car or mine?"

"Yours."

Baldrick covered his arms with his wings. "I'd almost forgotten how eternally cold my home is."

"You're right about that—I'm freezing!" The shivering dragon on the bird-man's shoulder squeezed himself into a tight ball.

"There's smoke coming out of the chimney," Fenright said. "We'll get nice and warm if your family will allow us to enter their home." He wrapped his arms about himself. "If I lived in this place, I'd have to start wearing clothes."

The bird-man nodded.

His family's stone-walled house stood alone on the flat, wild landscape. The wind blasting the moor was brutal; its unrelenting nature illustrated by the twisted trees growing at a permanently southern-pointing angle in the yard of the dwelling. The sky was heavy with thick, dark clouds whose only apparent purpose was to block the sunlight attempting to break through onto the cold earth below. All in all, this was a thoroughly inhospitable corner of the natural world.

"Can we go inside, please?" Fenright stamped his feet, which were becoming stiff. "I'm turning to ice from the bottom up!"

"Follow me." Baldrick walked up the rough stone pathway leading to the front door; the halfling close behind him. When he reached the entrance, he hesitated.

"Please hurry!"

The bird-man grasped the knob and twisted it. Opening the door, he poked his head inside. "Baldrick is here!"

"My son!" His mother stepped through a doorway. She was almost identical in appearance to her son, though her face was clearly feminine and the blue of her feathers paler than his. "I'm so happy you've come home!" She trotted towards him, stopping when she saw his companions. "What are these things doing here?"

"They're my friends."

"You can't bring undesirables into my home."

"Please, Mother. They'll freeze outside."

"That is not my problem!"

"I promised that you would allow them to stay here for a few days while we solve an important problem together. I promised, Mother! Would you make a liar out of your own son?"

"That important problem is yours; not mine. You may come inside, but the undesirables must leave.

What if someone sees them standing out there? What will become of my reputation?"

"We have no neighbors. Who is going to see them?"

"They must leave now. I shall not yield."

Baldrick stared into her eyes. "Neither shall I. Goodbye, Mother!" He slammed the door shut and turned to Fenright. "I'm so sorry. I thought I could persuade her to rise above her bigotry for my sake, but I was wrong."

"No need to apologize," Fenright said. "We should have put on false identities before you went to the door … it was our mistake." He hugged himself. "I can't stand it out here. Can you transport us to a warmer place?"

"Please." Verny lowered his head and whimpered.

"We need a building with heat and food," Baldrick said. "We need an unoccupied dwelling."

"Marit's home is empty and has plenty of food." Fenright squirmed. "It's quite warm inside, too!"

"I suppose she won't be returning soon, if at all. If she gets the ring, the Malvole will take it from her and kill her. If she doesn't get the ring and returns, I'll make a lot of trouble for her. Our Lord High Chief won't tolerate her breaking of the laws against violence."

"Please!"

"All right, Verny. Give me your hand, Fenright."

They vanished from the moor and appeared in Marit's home.

"Warmth!" The dragon left Baldrick's shoulder and landed on the floor before the radiator.

"Would you like some tea, sir?"

"Yes, thank you." The bird-man went to the bed and settled down. "We'll have one cup and then get started on the search for information. I have a knowledgable friend who can help us … does Marit have a phone?"

"It's on the bedside table behind you."

"Excellent."

Fenright turned to go into the kitchen area, then stopped and looked at Baldrick. "I keep wondering about something. The Malvole has killed quite a few creatures in his lifetime. He's accepted imprisonment in his house but has never been charged with a crime. Do you know why that is so?"

"He hasn't killed any purebreds, so due to his status as an aristocrat, our government has chosen leniency."

"I should have figured out that answer on my own." Fenright went into the kitchen. "I hope Jennifer's world doesn't operate like ours."

Baldrick picked up the phone receiver and pressed a button. "Could you connect me to Pharlap Knight's residence, please?" He waited a few moments. "Hello, Pharlap! How are you?" He grinned. "I'm good, thanks. I'll get directly to my reason for calling, if you don't mind. I'm looking for detailed information about the Malvole. What are his weaknesses? He's threatening some friends of mine and we need to know how to defend them." He listened for a moment. "I'll be there soon. Goodbye."

"Is your friend able to help?" Fenright stared at the kettle atop the stove.

"Yes, he has extensive documentation regarding Mr. Frinkland. I'm going there to pick it up."

"You don't want your tea first?"

"I'm too anxious to sit here waiting for the pot to boil. I'll have a cup when I return." He hopped off the bed. "My journey won't be an instantaneous affair. I want to exercise my wings, so I'll pop up onto the roof and fly to his home. He isn't far away."

"What will we do if Marit returns while you're gone?"

"Tell her if she harms you, shouts at you, or throws you out onto the street, I will go to the authorities, tell them what she's been doing in the other world, and they will deal with her. I'd like to do that now, but keeping Jennifer safe is more important."

"If those threats don't work," Verny said, "I can go after her face. It's her most valued possession … she wouldn't want my sharp claws marring her beauty."

"I didn't think you would ever fight back against her, no matter what she did." Fenright went to a cupboard and pulled out a package of tea. "What caused this change in you?"

"Baldrick defied his mother for our sakes. No one in this world has shown concern for me before today. He inspired me!" The dragon fluttered his wings and rose into the air; floating in the waves of heat above the radiator.

"I hope you won't have to engage in violent behavior, Verny. I'll be on my way now. See you soon!" The bird-man vanished.

Chapter 11

Baldrick crossed his arms over his chest and lifted off from the roof. Catching a rising air current, he soared over the city. The sun was sinking into the horizon; turning the sky pink and gold. Temperatures here were kinder than those at his family home, and the fresh air against his face was pleasing to him.

He looked at the streets below him, crowded with workers heading home at the end of their day. Cars, horse-drawn vehicles, and pedestrians packed the roads; all of them moving at a slow pace.

'It's a good thing not everyone can fly,' he thought. 'If the sky was congested like that, we'd all be crashing into one another.'

A tall spire of weathered stone poked up from amongst the brick and wooden buildings dominating the local architecture. He pointed himself toward the spire, slowed the beating of his wings, and began to lose altitude.

He landed before the iron-grilled entrance to Gryphyn Hall; one of the colleges of Norfam

University. Hundreds of years old and in need of restoration, the sprawling structure was composed of red brick with white stone facings. Through the grilled gateway, Baldrick could see the central green; crisscrossed with perfectly aligned paths left by a lawn mower.

He opened the gate and went to the half-doored opening to the office of the head page. Leaning over the top of the barrier, he put his head inside the room. "Hello!"

A man bearing a strong resemblance to a hedgehog scurried into view. "May I help you?"

"I'm here to see Professor Knight. My name is Baldrick Goforth. The professor is expecting me."

The human-shaped hedgehog picked up a book from a shelf near the door. Opening it, he perused a list of names and pencilled in a checkmark beside the bird-man's moniker. "I'll attend to the inner gate for you." He opened the door and went to the iron grille leading to the central yard. Using a large antique key, he unlocked the gate. "Do you know how to find Professor Knight's lodgings?"

"Yes, thank you."

"Have a good evening, sir." The page returned to his office.

Baldrick stepped onto the pavement surrounding the green and stopped to admire the interior of the college. Four levels of offices, flats, and meeting rooms rose up around him; each level possessing an open walkway edged with stone arches. Visible through the spaces between the arches, students and teachers clad in black robes hurried to and fro on their way to tutoring sessions.

The bird-man smiled. 'This is a lovely place,' he thought, 'full of eager youngsters, wise elders, and great heaps of knowledge.'

He climbed the stairs to the top floor and went to a door at the end of the passage. His knock was answered by a silver-haired man; his black robe hanging from his thin frame as though being worn by a skeleton.

"Pharlap, you really need to put on some weight!"

"I would if I had you cooking for me, instead of the barbarian who prepares our meals here." The professor smiled and stood aside to let Baldrick enter his lodgings. "Please, take a seat as best you can."

The bird-man settled down on a sofa. "Thank you for being willing to share your information with me."

"The pages are still printing out. There's over a hundred in total, and my printer isn't as fast as I'd like." Pharlap took a chair. "Have you been going on more expeditions to the other place?"

"Yes, I have."

"Have you learned anything I can add to the documentation?"

"There seem to be no advances in cultural or social progress, and I saw no evidence of scientific discoveries we're in a position to benefit from, I'm sorry to say."

"Why do you want information about Mr. Frinkland?"

"I have a good friend in the other world ..."

"You made contact! Wasn't that dangerous?"

"No, she's a nice lady and not inclined to spread the news of my presence."

"You'll learn more about her world through your friendship: that's good."

"As I was saying about my friend … Marit wants something of hers and has enlisted the aid of the Malvole in order to get it."

"Is she insane?" Pharlap leaned forward in his chair, mouth slightly open.

"Absolutely!"

"She's taken him out of his house?"

"Yes."

"She's broken the law. Are you going to the authorities about this?"

"I must protect my friend and can't get entangled in legal matters here. If you wish to pass the information on to law enforcement, I've no objections."

"I'll do that." The man rose from his chair. "The pages are finished printing. Let me get them into a box for you."

Back at Marit's home, Baldrick opened the box and took out the pages. "There has to be something in here that will enable us to save Jennifer," he said. "Can both of you read?"

"Yes!" the dragon and halfling stated in unison.

"I'll give you each a portion. Fenright, you can turn the pages for Verny. Let's get started."

Jennifer ran across the room to the pool-cue rack. "I'm getting them out of there before they run out of air, my poor babies."

"I don't think the closet is airtight."

"You think, but you don't know." She pushed the button to unlock the barrier. "Stand next to me so we can catch them if they try to run out."

They captured the nervous felines and got them into their carriers. With Basker at their heels, they carried the cats upstairs to the bedroom and released them.

Jennifer ran downstairs, grabbed the new pet supplies, and brought them into the room. Setting out a litter box, she filled it and slid it into a corner. Boris made for it right away.

"You shouldn't have gone downstairs alone," Ryan said. "We all have to stay together, remember?"

"I shouldn't have done that; it was stupid. Sorry … I won't make that mistake again." Sitting on the floor, the woman watched the cats move about the room as Basker lay before the closed bedroom door; head down on forelegs and eyes open. "I have no idea what we should do next."

"Same here." Ryan took a chair. "My war experience didn't prepare me for this kind of enemy. If they were ordinary humans, we could make a sound plan, but this ain't Vietnam."

"Thanks for serving there."

"You're welcome."

Jennifer reached out to Boris, and he climbed onto her lap. "Calling my bodyguards wouldn't help. I'd just be setting them up for death."

"Maybe. When we know more about the Malvole's limitations, it might turn out that they can deal with him."

"We know he can't invade our minds from a distance—if he could, he would've done it already. That's a good thing! He can only control us if he gets close. Also, he won't kill me because if he does, he won't get the ring. I think that's right, anyway. Does it make sense?" She rubbed her face with both hands. "My brain needs more blood."

Ryan lowered his head and stared at his shoes. "Maybe we need some coffee."

"We'll have to go through the whole thing with packing up the cats and putting them in the storage room again. I'm not leaving them in here while Basker escorts us to the kitchen."

"Yeah."

"Well, you know," Jennifer said, "what're the odds they're gonna pop in here, anyway? The Malvole is so terrified of Basker he won't go near him." She stroked the kitten's fur as he purred. "I'm kinda surprised Marit hasn't called to ask you what's taking so long."

"I didn't give her my number."

"You could call her and say you haven't had the chance to kill the dog yet, but you're working on it so they should just wait a bit longer."

"What if the Malvole gets into my brain through the phone?"

"Nah … even if he could, Basker would know and he'd take care of you right quick."

"Good point. I'll call her and buy us some time."

"Wait a sec. Does she have another gun?"

"I didn't see a weapon on her, but I can't guarantee she doesn't have one."

"If she gets tired of waiting for you to do the nasty deed, she might pop in and do it herself."

"She can try, but I have a lot more shooting experience than she does." Ryan reached behind himself and put a hand on the pistol tucked into the waistband of his pants.

"She has the element of surprise on her side."

"And I have the lightning-quick reflexes of a teenager."

"Maybe, when you call her, you can say I have my bodyguards again … the same ones who shot her. The memory of that ought to be enough to make her think twice about popping in here. Say they know where her heart is now."

"That would also provide me with an explanation as to why I haven't shot Basker yet. While those guys can't kill me, and she knows that, they'd be fast and strong enough to get the gun away from me if they saw me getting ready to use it."

"Yeah!" Jennifer crossed her legs. "Hurry up and call her so I can go to the bathroom alone, please."

Ryan pulled out his phone. It took a while for Marit to answer, as she wasn't familiar with the operation of cordless telephones. When she finally got on the line, he gave her all the details of the fictional situation. She accepted his story, made a few comments, and he put the phone away.

"They'll be content to wait a while. It seems the Malvole's become addicted to my vintage pinball machines and the Brie in my fridge."

"I think they suffer from a shortage of good cheese in their world. Baldrick had never encountered cheddar before, and he went crazy over it." Jennifer removed the kitten from her lap. Rising to her feet, she went into the bathroom attached to the sleeping chamber.

Ryan knelt beside Basker, scratching him around the ears as the dog's wagging tail slapped the floor. Natasha came out from under the bed, sat on her haunches before a window, and began to wash her face with her forepaws. Boris stretched out next to her and watched the feline perform her ablutions; his blue eyes open wide in fascination.

Jennifer emerged from the bathroom. "Shall we go down to the kitchen for coffee?"

"Sure."

"Let's keep the cats in here, even though we're safe for the moment. If they get loose in this huge house, we'll never be able to find them again."

Ryan put a hand on the door knob. "Basker, can you let me get out?" He pointed to the cats, and the hound rose and joined the felines. "Thanks, buddy."

"I'll take him out for a walk after we have some coffee."

"Good idea."

The pair left the room, closing the door behind them. Basker turned and went to a window. Pushing the curtains aside with his snout, he stared into the forest and growled.

"Goodbye, Ryan." Marit put down the phone and picked up the remote. She poked at its buttons, hissing every time her fingertips hit the squishy rubber pads. "I hate this thing! All these buttons with weird symbols that mean nothing to me! What is 'mode'?"

"Mode, mode, mode …" Mr. Frinkland wiggled his hips and shoulders, leaning backward and forward as he fought to raise the score displayed on the pinball's backglass. "I think mode is style or fashion."

"Why in the wawhozamites is there a button for fashion here?"

"Don't use foul language, Marit."

"Maybe if I push it, I'll be shown pictures of fine clothing." She pressed the button and glared at the television's big screen. "Nothing's happening!" She looked at the remote again and giggled. "Oh, I guess I need to use the power button."

Ryan had turned off the television days earlier after starting to watch a film on DVD, and it began to play. Putting her feet up on the coffee table, Marit settled into the couch cushions—a plate of chocolate cookies on her lap and bottle of beer in one hand—to watch an army of spear-bearing Greek warriors run across a Mediterranean beach. "This is wonderful." She put a cookie in her mouth and chewed; nodding with pleasure. "This is perfect."

Fenright turned over another page. "I haven't found anything useful yet. It's all quite interesting, but I'm not seeing any ways to control the Malvole."

"I'm not, either." Verny raised his head. "Can you flip this page over for me?" The halfling fulfilled his request.

"Keep reading, gentlemen," Baldrick said. "He has more weaknesses than a simple fear of animals. We will find them."

Gripping Basker's leash with both hands, Jennifer stepped out onto the front porch. The air was cool against her face: twilight had descended on the forest. Zipping up the jacket Ryan had loaned to her, she listened for signs of wildlife activity. The birds were quiet, but a soft rustling could be heard. She looked toward the sound, spotting a family of five raccoons scurrying through the underbrush.

"Don't even think about going after those guys, Basker."

He gazed into her eyes.

"I'm serious about that, you know."

They descended the stairs, and she decided to take the trail running through the trees at the north side of the house. As she walked the hound towards it, he stopped; turning his head to look behind them.

"I hope you haven't detected the presence of a mama bear with a cub. If you have, we're going back in the house." She turned to see what was attracting his interest. Something moved: a quick, silent shadow darting between the trees on the other side of the property. "That's not a bear, and it's not a deer. I don't know what it is, but I'm sure you can protect me from it. Let's check it out."

The dog led Jennifer across the driveway. At the edge of the forest, she stopped; holding the hound in place. "It's going to be a tight squeeze in there, but I think you're smart enough to not get yourself stuck between trees."

A low growl came from Basker's throat.

"Oh, dear."

Jennifer's body grew tense as an unearthly sound from the forest—an eerie combination of whining and hissing—made goosebumps rise up on her arms. The canine's growl increased in volume and intensity as his lips curled back, exposing his teeth in a vicious-looking snarl. He strained at the leash, and the woman tightened her grip.

"I don't think we should go in there." She tried to pull him back, but only succeeded in preventing him from moving forward. "Let's go, Basker."

Staring into the trees, he began to pant hot, deep breaths of ill-restrained rage that lent a weird rhythm to his amped-up growling.

"Come, Basker!" She tugged at the leash but he pulled it out of her grip, rose up on his hind legs, and howled.

As he dropped back down to earth, his call was answered by the whine-hiss of the creature hidden in the trees. A dark patch of shadow slid out from behind an oak trunk, moving towards them at warp speed.

Stopping within a foot of Basker, the shadow assumed a solid form. Draped in a loose wrapping of sackcloth, the creature's slimy exterior mirrored that of a golden garden slug. Its basic shape resembled a mollusk as well, though it had arms and legs and stood upright; equal to Jennifer's height. The tentacles topping the form wiggled and probed the air above something like a face with bulging black eyes and a lipless, jagged hole one could assume to be a mouth. The hole expanded a bit, and the awful hiss-whine erupted from it.

The woman froze, but but the hound did not. Lunging forward, he knocked the thing down and took off one of its arms with a single bite; spitting it out onto the ground.

The monster vanished.

Jennifer dropped down onto her hands and knees, gasping. "What in the hell was that?"

Chapter 12

"Ryan!" Basker leapt past the woman and ran into the house; his leash trailing behind him. She slammed the front door and locked it. "Ryan!"

He appeared in a doorway. "What?"

"Didn't you hear the howling and awful monster noise?"

"Double-paned windows throughout here … don't hear much of what goes on outside. What happened?"

"Not much … just a human-sized bipedal slug who ticked off Basker and lost an arm." Jennifer went to the nearest chair and plopped down. "It appeared to be some sort of Goer with an ability to move at high speed. It vanished after Basker bit off its arm." Tilting her head back, she shouted at the ceiling, "I hate this!"

"A bipedal slug? You mean it walked upright?"

"Yep."

"Seems physically impossible. I mean … slugs are kinda soft and squishy. How could a mollusk body stand upright without collapsing?"

"I looked at the arm it left behind and there was a green thing inside that looked like a bone made out of hard rubber. I think there were muscles, too, but I really didn't want to spend a lot of time examining it."

"Did you get the impression the thing's dangerous?"

"Basker did, and that's good enough for me." She leaned forward. "He's running around dragging his leash; he can get hurt. Basker, come!" The hound ran into the room, and she removed the leash. He galloped away and ran up the staircase. "He pooped after the monster left, so I guess he's good for a few more hours. Next time, you can take him outside … please."

"I wonder if it's possible to kill a giant slug with a bullet? I have a feeling it isn't. I mean … a hail of bullets might do it, but there are only ten in my gun. I don't have any more than that, and I don't want to waste them." Ryan stared at the floor; pondering the situation. "I know—I've got a good supply of fire extinguishers here, what with the fire department being far away. We can take out a mollusk with those. They have potassium bicarbonate as the active agent, which is salty. Salt kills slugs."

"That's an excellent idea!" She leaned back in the chair. "I can't believe we're discussing how to kill giant slugs."

"We need to be prepared in case more of them show up. Basker's quick, but I don't know how he'd handle an army of … giant, fast-moving slugs." He shook his head. "This is so unbelievable, it's almost funny."

"If you'd met it, you wouldn't find it amusing."

"Yeah, it's just that your description reminds me of the kinds of things I used to see in cheesy horror movies when I was a kid."

"I don't understand why such a creature would show up here. Stands to reason it was after the ring, but I don't think it had the facility for speech, so it wouldn't be able to recite the formula."

"Did the arm have a hand with fingers?"

"Yes; fat, slimy fingers that would smear the ink you used to write down the words."

"Guess the creature doesn't know what's required to make the ring work."

She shook her head. "I don't understand how Goers manage to find what they're looking for; landing in just the right place when they haven't been there before. I can kinda get the idea of using mental powers to get through dimensional barriers, but that other stuff mystifies me. The illogicality is irritating."

"I expect the process is logical, but since we don't understand how it works, it appears not to be. I suppose thousands of years ago, people looked at the sun and remarked upon the illogicality of a ball of fire hanging in the sky and never burning out."

"Yeah." Jennifer stood and unzipped her jacket. "What the heck … might as well get on with life. I suppose we should sleep in shifts tonight."

"Yes." He headed for the entrance to a corridor. "I'll get the extinguishers and put 'em someplace handy, then we can feed the animals and have dinner."

Mr. Frinkland stood before Marit; a plate of crackers and blue-veined cheese in his hands. "I believe that beverage you've been drinking is having a negative effect upon you." He sat beside her.

"Huh?" She opened her eyes. Her bare feet, still atop the coffee table, were surrounded by empty beer bottles.

"It's either that or the cookies."

"The package is printed with a statement declaring that milk loves these cookies, which doesn't make any sense. How can milk love anything?"

"May I have one?"

"If you like."

He picked up the package sitting on the table and put his hand inside. "It's empty."

"I couldn't stop eating them."

"Do they possess any nutritional value?"

"I don't know. There's information on the wrapper, but I didn't read it." She closed her eyes.

He picked up one of the bottles, sniffed the opening, and raised his upper lip in an expression of disgust. "It smells like something perished and decomposed in there."

"You're exaggerating. It tastes good, and it's fizzy."

"It's probably what has made you act so odd. You speak as if the action's a great effort, and your eyes drift when they're open." He leaned in close to her. "Look at me."

She followed the instruction.

"Oh! Your eyes are looking in two different directions! That's horrible!"

She closed them. "I don't feel very good."

"I'll get you a glass of water." He rose and walked towards the kitchen; stopping when he heard a retching sound. Turning, he saw Marit leaning to one side; vomiting up cookies and beer. "I'm not cleaning that up!"

The woman moaned. "I'll get to it later."

He went into the kitchen and returned with a glass of water. "Drink this."

She guzzled it down. A moment later, it came back up her throat and spilled all over her lap.

"This is the most disgusting display I have ever witnessed."

"Do you think the purpose of this beverage is to clean out a person's digestive tract?" She burped. "Sorry. I have to admit, vomiting made me feel much better."

"I suppose it's possible, but you'd think with the advanced science they have in this world, they'd be able to come up with a medication that would do that in a more economical manner; as in not requiring the consumer to drink twelve bottles in order to obtain the benefit."

"Maybe one is supposed to drink only one bottle and then wait an hour." She burped again. "Sorry. Perhaps it's a matter of time; not volume."

"Perhaps." He took a chair a good distance away from the malodorous spillages. "I hope this won't impair your transporting abilities. Ryan should be calling anytime now to tell us it's safe for me to get close to the woman."

"Sogolog is watching them; don't forget about that." She removed her feet from the table, knocking over four of the empty bottles. "I need to find some clean clothes." Rising halfway off the couch, she quickly sat down again and leaned back; her head resting on the sofa. "My coordination is impaired, and I feel a sense of vertigo."

"I'll get something to replace your dirty gown." He headed for a hallway. "It's unfortunate that the people in this world have no sense of style whatsoever. I'll probably find nothing but rags in that man's closet."

"Uh, huh." Marit closed her eyes.

A few minutes later, he came back into the room. "I managed to find garments made from fabrics with texture and color. They're quite nice!" Smiling, he held up a purple-brocade dressing gown and set of green-satin pajamas. "I hope you don't mind wearing trousers. They're too big for you, but they have an adjustable waist."

"Uh, huh." She sighed, tipped to one side, and passed out.

He set the clothes on the end of the couch. Going to Marit, he poked her shoulder. "Wake up!" There was no response, so he poked again. "Are you dead?" Listening, he detected the sound of her breathing. "You're not dead. What's wrong with you?" He stepped back and glared at her.

"Mr. Frinkland." The voice was like a thick fluid splattering on cement.

"Ah!" He turned to see the one-armed slug. "Sogolog, you startled me!"

"I apologize, sir." His black eyes regarded the collapsed woman. "What is wrong with Miss Bonderditch?"

"I'm not certain, but I suspect her unconsciousness is caused by overconsumption of the fluid that was in those empty bottles." He pointed at the glass vessels on the table.

"What is that vile odor?"

"Her stomach ejected its contents all over her lap and the furniture." He looked at the visitor's side. "Where is your arm?"

"I left it behind at the dwelling of the ring's owner."

"Are you in pain?"

"I feel mild discomfort. A new limb will grow from the wound in a short time."

"Have you any activity to report?"

"The woman was outside with the dog, who was alarmed by my presence and removed my limb." The slug touched the open wound. "I attempted to intimidate him with my voice, which was a mistake."

"There were no humans with her?"

"None."

Raising a hand, the Malvole fingered one of the pearls adorning his beard. "It seems odd to me that she would go outside without at least one of her bodyguards. But then … perhaps she considered the dog to be adequate protection."

"He is a force to be regarded with respect; that is certain."

"I'm tired of waiting for Ryan to kill that animal. Can you get a gun and shoot him for me? You could stand outside a window and fire through the glass so he can't injure you again."

"My hands aren't good at working with mechanical devices. Miss Bonderditch can do that for you when she recovers from the effects of the substance she ingested." He glanced at the unconscious woman. "That is, if she recovers. Maybe she will die?"

The Malvole picked up an empty beer bottle and read the label. "There's nothing written on here indicating a potential for immediate fatality due to overconsumption of the contents." He set the bottle down and poked Marit's shoulder. "Are you feeling better?" he shouted.

Eyes still closed, she opened her mouth and uttered a few incomprehensible words.

"I think she's going to be all right. We can just wait, I suppose." He smiled at Sogolog. "I'd offer you a seat, but …"

"Yes, I do tend to leave residue on anything I touch. I'll go outside and lie on the grass. Please let me know when Miss Bonderditch wakes up."

"Will do." Mr. Frinkland watched Sogolog walk towards the sliding-glass door leading to the backyard. Each step he took with his big, flat, webbed feet left a spot of slime on the carpet. "I'm not cleaning that up!"

Ryan took a bowl of vegetable soup out of the microwave and set it before Jennifer. "This is pretty good for canned stuff. Put some of the hot sauce in it … that'll mask the processed taste."

"Thanks."

"Do you want some chips with that?"

"If they're potato, yes."

He extracted a bag from a kitchen cupboard, opened it and set it on the table. "Do you want mineral water or soda?"

"Water, please."

He grabbed two bottles of water from the fridge. "Here ya go."

"Thanks." She waited until he was seated, then picked up her spoon. "Can I ask you a moderately personal question?"

"Sure!"

"What did you do for a living before you got your fortune?"

"I own an auto-repair shop."

"Do you still work there?"

"I drop in now and then to hang out with the guys."

"Don't they wonder how you got young again?"

"I told them the truth. Took a while to convince them I'm really me, but they're cool with it now."

"So you just went around telling everyone you had a magic ring?"

"I was careful about it; only told people I trust."

"Marit said you had trouble finding anyone you could trust after you got rich; that's why you gave the ring to me instead of someone you already knew."

"That's not true. I wanted to give it to someone who was not only kind, but needed a break. All my friends and relatives were pretty well set up, so they didn't need it." He swallowed a spoonful of soup. "After I used my last wish, I decided to give the ring to the first person I encountered who fit that profile. When I saw you get out of that old wreck you were driving to rescue the kitten, I figured you were the right one." He smiled. "I think I made a good choice. You didn't go crazy with the ring's power and make foolish decisions, and I know for certain you won't use for anything malicious."

"I appreciate your faith in me." She grabbed a handful of chips. "You don't have a wife or kids?"

"Ex-wife; two grown sons. One's an attorney; the other designs software."

"Do they live near you?"

"Sam's in New York and Joe moved to Oregon a few months ago."

"Have you had a good life so far?"

"Yeah, things have gone along pretty well for me. My parents were great people, and so is my brother. My divorce wasn't too bad; we both agreed that we'd grown too far apart. No fights or anything like that."

"I'm glad to hear it."

"How about you? What's your life been like?"

"Well, I'm alive."

"I guess that's something!" He took a swig of water from the bottle. "Not good, then?"

"Some good; some bad. My parents were wonderful, but they died in a car crash when I was nineteen. They were driving back to Montana to visit relatives, and it appeared that my father fell asleep at the wheel and the car went over a cliff."

"I'm so sorry." He shook his head. "That's terrible."

"Yeah." She bit her lower lip. "I dropped out of college after it happened. Mom and Dad left me a little money and I survived on that until I found a job. The rent on our apartment was pretty high and I had to move to a cheaper place. I couldn't afford to hire movers, so I left all our furniture behind. Things got really tough for a long time, and then … I had some bad experiences with criminals that I really don't want to talk about." Her gaze darted to a corner of the kitchen, then she looked back at Ryan. "Can we change the subject?"

"Let's talk about your new life. How are you handling being on the top-ten-richest list?"

"It's working out okay so far. I delete the emails I get from strangers, and I turn on my landline for just a few hours a day. People who try to call me when it's turned off get a ringing tone that never stops, which I think serves as a deterrent."

"If you ever decide to have an active social life, you can get a secretary who'll filter the communications for you."

"Fenright and Baldrick are too busy with their chores as it is, and Verny can't pick up a phone, so I'd have to hire someone new who could tolerate my roommates. That would be difficult."

"Yes, it would." Ryan nodded. "Are you at least enjoying your incredible bank balance?"

"I haven't had much of a chance to enjoy it, but for that brief period of time when I thought Marit would stay away from me; yeah, that was nice."

"Do you want to take another shot at wishing her away?"

She shook her head. "It would be too dangerous. As soon as I get the ring out of the lockbox, it'll be vulnerable to Marit and that monster showing up and stealing it before I can make the wish. That would be the end of our world as we know it."

"I suppose so."

"Until this matter with Marit and the Malvole is resolved, the ring stays locked up. I'm not going to change my mind about that."

"Okay."

"I just wish … ack! Baldrick, you scared me!"

"Sorry, Jennifer." He let go of Fenright's hand.

Verny left the bird-man's shoulder and floated into the air. "We have news!"

Baldrick set the box of papers on the kitchen table. "We found a method of protection from the Malvole's powers." He smiled. "If you have a way to emit compressed air from a pneumatic device that can put out a deafening noise, it disrupts certain circuits in his brain and renders him unable to perform."

"An air horn?" Ryan laughed. "Those can render everyone unable to perform!"

"He does need to be rather close to the device for it to work, but it's better than nothing."

"How long does the effect last?"

"The documentation regarding the Malvole doesn't mention that."

"I can get those horns at a sporting-goods store. If I move fast, I can get to the local one before they close."

"Move fast, then," Jennifer said, "and take your gun with you just in case. We'll stay here."

Ryan jogged out of the kitchen. "See ya later!"

Baldrick looked at the dishes on the table. "I must wash those."

"No, leave them. Come upstairs with me so we can all stay together with the animals." She rose from her chair. "Are you guys hungry?"

"We ate at Marit's home."

"What were you doing there?"

"We needed a warm place to read the documentation."

"Okay."

Baldrick grabbed the box, and the group went upstairs to join the animals. As soon as the bedroom door was opened, Boris galloped to meet Fenright, who picked him up and cuddled him. "Nice to see you again, kitten," he whispered into the cat's ear.

Everyone settled down except the tiny dragon, who floated over the assembly. "It's good to be back," Verny said. "We were not well received by Baldrick's mother." He slowed the beating of his wings and landed on the halfling's shoulder.

"What happened?" Jennifer asked.

"She refused to let us stay; ordering Fenright and me to get off her land at once because we're undesirables."

"Oh, your world's caste system."

"I'm ashamed of my mother's behavior. I'm so sorry I allowed you two to be humiliated like that."

"Don't apologize, Baldrick," the halfling said. "Your mother was simply adhering to society's rules."

"Do all the beings who're discriminated against have your forgiving attitude, Fenright?" Jennifer shook her head. "That's not right . . . you need to resist that system."

"Baldrick resisted it and no longer enjoys a good relationship with his family."

"I don't mind that," the bird-man said. "My separation from them has been building up for a while."

"Does your world hold elections?"

"Yes, but only purebreds are allowed to vote."

Jennifer sighed. "I'm surprised you all have the ability to read. Is that legal in your world, or are you breaking the laws?"

"The purebreds decided it's advantageous to have servants who can read, so they granted us that right some years ago. We are allowed to be educated up to a certain level, though we aren't permitted to attend universities."

"I'm beginning to understand why you don't resist the system. You could get hurt or killed, I imagine."

"The Malvole hasn't been convicted of murder for the beings he killed because none of them were purebreds," Fenright said, "so, yes; we would suffer the ultimate punishment if we show any signs of resistance."

"That makes me sick." Jennifer clasped her hands; squeezing them tight. She was silent for a few moments, then cleared her throat. "With your guidance, gentlemen, I'd like to use one of my wishes to bring an end to your world's horrible status quo."

"Really?" Verny hopped down onto the floor and looked up at the woman. "You'd do that for us?"

"You need to explain to me what changes should be made in order for the wish to work correctly. I can't just say, 'I wish for freedom for all beings of Euromoss.' Maybe the ring's power would decide that killing everybody off would be a good way to do it; you know what I mean?" She released her hands and stretched her fingers. "If I tried to do something like that for my world, the challenge of rising above my emotions while ensuring that nothing would go catastrophically wrong would overwhelm me."

"You need something like that here?" Fenright asked.

"I've read this world's newspapers," Baldrick said, "and they do need something like that."

Jennifer rose from her chair and began to pace; hands clasped behind her back. "Yeah, I'm gonna do this. No more sitting around waiting for Marit to play her hand … as soon as Ryan gets back, we're going after the bad guys and putting them out of commission so I can get to the ring safely and remove the yoke from you and your kind." She stopped pacing and looked at the bird-man. "You told me that just about everyone in your world looks down on someone. Does that mean I'll have to change the attitudes of everyone except the beings at the very bottom of the heap?"

"I'll have to think about that."

"Okay; no rush."

Followed by Basker, Baldrick went to a window and looked outside. "How about I go spy on Marit to see what she's up to?"

"I don't know where Ryan's other home is, so we'd need to wait for him to get back so he can give you directions."

"I'll take Verny with me—he can serve as a connection to lead me to Marit. He lived with her long enough to form a bond."

"How does that work, anyway? How do you know where to go without a map … in fact, how do you guide yourself even when you have a map?"

"It's impossible to put the process into words."

"Okay." Jennifer nodded. "Oh, I forgot to tell you: there was a giant slug here that seemed to be a Goer."

"A giant slug?"

"Yeah, a human-sized slimy golden slug that stood upright and has two arms and two legs. Well, it only has one arm now—Basker tore the other one off."

"That's probably Sogolog," Fenright said, "or a member of his gang."

"You mean there's a bunch of creatures just like him that go around wreaking havoc together?"

"They perform unpleasant tasks purebreds don't want to do themselves and get paid for it," Baldrick said.

"I hope he doesn't decide to bring his friends here to help him harass us. Are they violent?"

"If they're paid to hurt someone, they are."

"Are they all Goers that can move at lightning speed like the guy I saw?"

"Yes."

"I see. Well, I'm sure you'll be careful and not allow anyone to see you while you're at Ryan's place."

"We might as well go right now. Come on, Verny."

The dragon flew onto his shoulder, and the pair disappeared.

Chapter 13

Baldrick swooped over the house, holding the dragon against his chest. "This is the place. See Sogolog sitting down there on the back lawn?"

"I trust you will avoid his slimy company."

"He's getting up and heading for the house. Let's wait until he goes inside."

The bird-man circled the property, staying at a height that would prevent Sogolog from hearing the sound of his wings beating the air. When the moist creature entered the building, he landed on the grass a hundred feet from the back windows.

Verny climbed onto his shoulder. "Nice of them to leave the curtains open."

"Yes. If we stay in the shadows, we can get close without being seen."

Lights attached to the back of the house shed a bright illumination over the yard, but trees here and there offered dark hiding places to the two winged creatures. Baldrick tiptoed forward, staying in the shadows, as Verny crept along beside him.

"Stop here," the bird-man whispered.

Looking through the sliding-glass doors, they peered into the room. Marit lay on her side on the couch; eyes closed and mouth open.

"She looks dead," Verny said.

"She might be."

"Look at all those bottles. I guess they put away a lot of soda."

"Sogolog's just staring down at the floor and not moving."

"The Malvole's in the corner standing in front of a thing with lots of blinking colored lights." Verny watched for a moment. "Do you think it's the command center of some kind of war machine?"

"The images at the back are representations of automobiles, so I … I'm not sure. I don't think low-slung cars have anything to do with the military in this world."

"You think, but you don't know."

"We should go back and report this to Jennifer." He leaned down and picked up Verny.

They rematerialized in the bedroom.

"Yikes! You need to send some kind of warning signal to let me know when you're coming!"

"Sorry, Jennifer—that's not possible."

"I was just kidding."

"We couldn't tell exactly what's going on at Ryan's house. The Sogolog was there, just standing inside doing nothing. Marit was lying on the couch; dead or sleeping."

"There were many bottles on the table beside her," Verny said.

"Bottles, eh? What did they look like?"

"They were made of brown glass and the same size as soda bottles."

"Did you see any labels?"

"One of them said, 'guyness.'

"That would be Guinness, which explains Marit's state. She got drunk and passed out."

"How does one get drunk? Only beverages get drunk."

"What?"

"How do you drink a person? Even if that were possible, she's intact and lying on the couch, so obviously no one drank her."

Jennifer stared at the dragon.

"He has a point, you know," Baldrick said.

"Oh, I get it, I think." She nodded. "You don't have alcohol in your world."

"We have alcohol. It's used to clean wounds and dissolve chemicals."

"No one drinks it?"

"Do you think we're insane?"

"We drink it here. When a person drinks enough to get intoxicated, we refer to them as being drunk."

"Intoxication is poisoning!"

"No, it's not!"

"What does 'toxic' mean to you?"

"Poisonous."

"My point exactly!"

She let out a loud sigh. "This conversation's going nowhere. Let's just come to an agreement about Marit: she consumed a fluid that rendered her temporarily unconscious. Can you accept that?"

"Yes."

"How about you, Verny?"

"I will accept that."

"Thank you."

Baldrick folded his legs and settled on the floor. "We're concerned about the Malvole's activity. He was standing in front of a device with flashing lights which Verny thought might be the controls of a military device."

"Ryan's not a member of the military, so that seems unlikely." Jennifer frowned. "Oh, that might've been one of his pinball machines. Were there pictures on it?"

"Yes, colorful images of low-slung cars."

"Yeah, that's a pinball machine. It's a big toy; nothing to worry about."

Thumping footsteps approached the door. Ryan entered the room; a large bag in one hand. "I got air horns!"

Basker rose and went to meet the man. He sniffed the bag, wagged his tail, and lay down before the closed door.

"How many did you get?" Fenright asked.

"I got one for everybody who has hands, so that came to a total of four."

"I have hands," Verny said.

"Well, yeah, but they're tiny."

"True."

Jennifer used her hands and eyes to make a come-here suggestion to Natasha, who was lying beside Fenright; watching as he stroked Boris. The tabby went to the woman and climbed onto her lap. "I suppose we should get prepared and go do our stuff."

"What do you mean by 'go do our stuff'?" Ryan asked.

"She decided," Baldrick said, "that she wants to get the villains out of the picture immediately so she can use the ring to change our world into a more balanced place."

"More balanced?"

"They need to get their civil rights straightened out." Jennifer scratched behind the tabby's ears. "Only purebred humans can vote, and there are other serious problems as well."

"So their world's the way our country was when I was a child."

"If you want to consider that situation to be something in our past, go for it."

"Yeah. Well … fixing their situation sounds good to me, so let's do our stuff, which I assume means some kind of attack."

"Yes. Marit drank a bunch of your Guinness Stout and passed out, so if we move quickly, we won't have to worry too much about her. We've got the fire extinguishers for dealing with slug monsters, so that shouldn't be a problem, but how do we deal with the

Malvole? I'm assuming continuous blasts from the air horns will only get us so far in controlling him."

"We'll need to render him unconscious. I hate the idea of pounding on an unarmed man's head until he blacks out—I might kill him doing that. There has to be a better way."

"He's not unarmed," Fenright said. "He can control your mind and kill any of us with a single thought."

"Google how to make someone unconscious safely," Jennifer said.

Ryan pulled out his phone and went online. "Let's see …" His companions watched in silence as he stared at the screen, going from one site to another.

After a couple of minutes, he put the phone away. "This ain't gonna happen. I'd need to be a trained nurse or doctor and have access to needles and the right drug; that's the only way to put someone out without messing them up."

"You might want to remember," Baldrick said, "that the creature in question is a murderer. He's killed quite a few mixed breeds. I personally would have no problem with whacking him over the head until he goes down."

"We're planning to take out a giant slug using a method that will probably kill him … I don't see why we should give preferential treatment to the Malvole." Jennifer frowned.

Ryan looked up at the ceiling and sighed. "I killed people during the war and really don't want to do it again," he said; his voice almost a whisper. "While I'm willing to shoot Marit in self-defense, stalking the

Malvole with the intention of killing him feels too much like murder."

"I'll knock him out," the bird-man said. "Don't worry about it."

Ryan nodded.

"So … we take out the slug-thing and the Malvole while Marit's sleeping off the stout. What next?" Jennifer nibbled on a fingernail.

"Baldrick can take them home," Fenright said. " Perhaps you should take them directly to the constables' headquarters? You can do that, right?"

"I can and will."

"Three big creatures like that seems like quite a load for one Goer. Can you handle it?"

"I can only manage two large beings at once. We can deal with that at the end of the battle … perhaps not all three villains will survive?"

"That is possible," Jennifer said.

"Ow! What's that?" Baldrick lifted one big clawed bird-foot to avoid whatever was poking at the sole of it. "Ah!" He stepped back as a chunk of what appeared to be foliage broke through the floor beneath him.

The unexpected bit of greenery shot up to the ceiling of the room and ceased moving, having brought a mass of branches and a truly gigantic tree trunk along with it.

"Uh …" Ryan stared at the treetop.

"Smells good!" Jennifer giggled. "I love the scent of redwood; oh, yeah …" She closed her eyes and drew in a big deep snort of *Sequoia sempervirens* perfume, then leaned forward and tried to hug the ten-foot diameter trunk.

"What in the hell is this thing doing here?"

Jennifer leaned into the tree's fragrant bark. "Oh, I like this; um, oh, yeah." She pressed her nose against the furry red surface of the monster redwood.

The cats bolted and hid under a bed. Basker sat back on his haunches and barked. Everyone else stood transfixed in silence, staring at the unexpected intrusion.

A branch began to wiggle like an angry snake. It stretched out, wrapped itself around Jennifer, grabbed her, and pulled her into a close embrace against the tree trunk. A knothole beside the branch's base opened and the limb pushed the woman into it. The hole closed and the branch straightened out, resuming its normal position.

Ryan raised his hands into the air. "What in the hell?"

Baldrick shook his head as a garbled sound came from his throat.

Fenright rubbed his hands together. "I absolutely do not know what to say."

Verny rose into the air and circled the tree. "Is this a normal occurrence in this world?"

"It is not." Ryan lowered his arms.

"Shall we force our way through that knothole to rescue Jennifer?"

"Well, yeah … I guess so."

"Look out, Verny!" Baldrick stepped back. "The tree is sinking!"

The tiny dragon flew away from the mass of branches as the treetop made a rapid descent towards earth and vanished into it. A second later, it popped right back up, the knothole opened and ejected Jennifer onto one of the beds, and the gigantic plant sank bank into the earth.

She sat up and shook her head. "Whoa!" Boris ran out from his hiding place and jumped onto her lap. She stroked his head and let out a deep breath. "Okay; that was really weird."

"What was with the tree-hugging?" Ryan asked.

"I don't know. I just felt a great big rush of affection for it. I do love redwoods."

"Yeah, but that response in that situation was pretty peculiar."

"Maybe."

"Are you okay?" Fenright asked.

"Yeah. I feel kind of odd, but … I don't feel bad. Just slightly, well; more solid than my usual self. And I've got a weird new idea stuck in my head which I'll keep to myself for now."

Ryan stared at the damage to his floor. "I wonder if my insurance will pay for this."

"Do you have acts of God coverage?"

"Don't remember; I think I do." He shrugged. "Maybe we should relocate to another room before somebody falls through that hole and gets hurt."

"Good idea." Jennifer picked up Boris, Fenright got Natasha, and the group moved to a different bedroom.

"I don't see much point in trying to figure out why a redwood came up out of nowhere and snatched me up. That mystery is best pondered at some point in the distant future." The woman sat in a chair and stroked the kitten. "Where were we before the tree interrupted us?"

"We were about to go to my other house with our supply of unorthodox weapons."

"Someone needs to stay here to look after my pets in case something awful happens and we lose the battle."

"Fenright can do that."

"Yes, he can." She smiled at the halfling. "I'll give you Brett's phone number so you can call him if needs be."

"I've never operated a telephone machine."

"I'll teach you—it's easy."

"Thank you, ma'am."

"Verny, you should stay here. I don't want you to get hurt."

"Yes, ma'am."

Chapter 14

Baldrick, Ryan, and Jennifer appeared at the far edge of the lawn behind the house. They had decided to use the bird-man's Goer abilities instead of a car due to the desirably silent and speedy aspects of his form of travel.

"Okay." Ryan held a bag of air horns in each hand. "Let's figure out how to proceed."

Jennifer hugged the load of fire extinguishers she held in her arms. "Let's see … you can barge in with an air horn blaring so Baldrick is free to pound on the Malvole's head while I go at the slug thing with my fire extinguisher. I think I should, um, whack Marit over the head with my fire extinguisher before I start spraying the slug, just to make sure she doesn't wake up too soon."

"Sounds like a good plan." Ryan nodded.

"And then, when they're all incapacitated to one degree or another, Baldrick can haul them off one at a time to the law enforcement establishment of his home town. Does that sound right to you, Baldrick?"

"Oh, sure. Knock 'em out; haul 'em off. That should work out fine."

"We should go in through one of the entrances at the side of the house, so we can creep towards them from inside the building rather than using one of the glass doors where they can see us coming." Ryan took a step forward. "Follow me."

They entered the house and crept silently through hallways, pausing outside a small library so Ryan could retrieve a fireplace poker from within. When they reached the room containing the villains. Ryan grasped the doorknob of the entrance. Taking a deep breath, he turned the knob, opened the door, and fired off one of the air horns.

The Malvole—standing over the recumbent Marit—moaned, dropped his head down, and covered his ears with both hands. The slug-man, lurking in a far corner, used his talent for rapid movement to instantly bring himself to Ryan's side. It reached for the air horn as Jennifer sprayed the thing's face and upper body with a fire extinguisher.

Sogolog shrieked. The outer layers of his viscous yellow hide began to bubble and melt; his forehead dripping down over his hideous black eyes. Jennifer recoiled at the sight and continued to direct the chemicals from the container onto the creature, hoping the thing would dissolve and disappear in a mercifully short period of time. It did proceed to decompose at a rapid pace, so she persisted in spraying the chemicals onto the creature.

Marit groaned. Rubbing her face with both hands, she rose to a seated position on the couch and focused her gaze on the melee. "What is going on?" She stood up, staggering a bit.

Sogolog was no longer a threat, so Jennifer ran to the woman and hit her over the head with a fire extinguisher. The assault had the desired effect: Marit fell back down onto the couch in a semi-conscious state. "Baldrick! Can you get her out of here?"

The bird-man was busily whacking away at the Malvole's head with the poker. The man had gone down, kneeling on the floor while trying to protect his skull with both arms.

"Isn't he unconscious yet?" Jennifer yelled.

"This isn't easy!" Baldrick continued to whack away.

Ryan dropped the air horn he'd been using and picked up a fresh one; resuming the emitting of the ear-splitting noise that was keeping the Malvole somewhat subdued.

"Let me help!" Jennifer leapt over the coffee table and began to kick away at the Malvole's head. "Damn, it's hard to knock someone out!" She kicked away as the villain continued to shield his skull with his hands and arms.

Out of nowhere came the sound of voices; voices so loud that they drowned out the shriek of the air horn. Ryan stopped pressing the button of his device as he turned to look at the source of the vocalizations.

A group of four dark-haired young women with black-feathered wings sprouting from their backs stood inside the room. Their bodies were covered in dark purple feathers, and they wore heavy gold chains around their necks which sat at the line where the feathers gave way to pale human skin.

A group of eight men in formal black suits and top hats stood behind them, gazing intently at the Malvole as the women sang a chant of abstract sounds that mimicked the noise of ocean-borne winds sucking through a cave by the sea. In and out the sound went; a piercing, howling wail that made the humans in the room shiver.

The eight men broke into two groups. Stepping forward with quiet, calm purpose; they quickly wrapped heavy lead chains around Marit and the Malvole. When the male villain was securely chained, a man secured a sort of sack made from lead chain mail over his head.

The sirens ceased their singing and each one took the hand of one of the men. The other four men put their hands on Marit and the Malvole, and the entire assembly vanished.

"Yeah!" Jennifer laughed. "That was great!"

"Wow!" Ryan said. "A totally effective apprehension of the bad guys achieved with no firearms whatsoever. That's terrific!"

"That was a lot easier than I expected it to be. In the movies, people always have to fight battles for a long time before they win. You kinda get to thinking everything has to go on for a certain number of beats before anything can get accomplished."

"Yeah, like how movie cops always have to throw themselves against a door three times before they can break it down."

"Drives me nucking futs."

"Me too."

"Fortunately, real life doesn't have to adhere to tropes and cliches and nonsensical rules."

"Yeah."

Baldrick studied the heap of decomposed slug-stuff. "Let's go for some ice cream, okay?"

"Yeah, ice cream, and then we can figure out how to save your world. We'll take care of that after I deal with the bizarre idea that's been in my head since the tree snatched me and spit me out again." Jennifer took one of the bird-man's hands, Ryan took the other, and they vanished.

A few days later, the gang assembled in Jennifer's living room. She had acquired a gigantic television screen which hung on the wall before a collection of cushions, sofas, and comfy chairs. A secret surprise event had been arranged; one which Jennifer said they could watch on the new TV.

Bowls of buttered popcorn were distributed. When everyone was seated, Jennifer picked up the remote and switched on the TV. After a little searching, she found the news broadcast she was looking for.

The transmission showed the President of the United States struggling to move his overweight body up a short flight of stairs to a podium. When he reached the dais, he jutted his head forward and forced out a toothy grin. Raising one hand in the air to salute the crowd in a gesture unfortunately similar to an appalling one from humanity's recent past, he opened his mouth and shouted, "I made America great again! I did it; I am the only one who could …" He choked, and his red face changed to deep scarlet. The orange hair atop his head stood straight up, and he began to slowly spin round and round. His stature lessened, his clothing collapsed as his body rapidly shrank down to a diminutive size.

As the world watched, the POTUS was transformed into a wasp. The buzzing insect jerked back and forth in a crazed orbit around the microphone, then flew away to parts unknown.

Jennifer collapsed into laughter. "I'm evil and I don't care! This is the best day of my life!"

Ryan and Brett let out screams of hilarity and fell onto the floor, rolling and kicking with glee. Verny soared into the air. "I like that; I like that!" he cried.

"Oh, dear," Fenright muttered, breaking into a guilty smile.

"I need more salt for my popcorn." Maldrick giggled as he trotted towards the kitchen.

It was fine, fine day in America.

FINIS

I'm so pleased that you took the time to read my little story. If you are so inclined, it would be great if you could post a brief review at the site where you acquired this book or at Goodreads. Have a great day!

OTHER WORKS BY D.L. LEWIS

WHERE WOLVES TALK (Volume 1)
A Fantasy for Animal Lovers

FINALE (Volume 2 of the Where Wolves Talk Duology)

STEPHEN KING IS WRONG—A Supernatural Thriller

DOPPELGÄNGER—A Tragicomic Novella

FIGHTING BACK—A Brief Memoir

53005111R00136

Made in the USA
San Bernardino, CA
03 September 2017